a lowercase hell

By Gerald Dean Rice

Print Edition

Copyright 2024 Red Hand Books

a lowercase hell

Other available titles...

The Devil's Gunt

Dead 'til Dawn

*Absolute Garbage, Total Nonsense, & Utter
Ridiculousness*

a lowercase hell

Gerald Dean Rice

a lowercase hell:
What goes down will try to come up.

"No good deed goes unpunished."
—Some Douchebag

"You look pretty good down here,
But you ain't really good"
—Harry Styles

"We're just ordinary people
We don't know which way to go
'Cause we're ordinary people
Maybe we should take it slow
Take it slow, ohhh
This time we'll take it slo-o-o-o-oooooow"
—John Legend

Prologue: Your Cursed Penis and You

Median awoke from what had to have been a nightmare. There was no way a nurse had just…It wasn't possible someone had had her hand on his…

He lifted the covers and checked. Of course, he still had his penis. The nightmare hadn't been someone ripping it off. He couldn't help feeling for himself, though, nodding once he'd confirmed it was still attached.

Median wasn't sure he could sleep in this room another night. He was afraid the nightmare might be more than a nightmare. There were shadows in here where shadows didn't belong. He swore shapes in the darkness would move if he didn't watch constantly.

And someone had put a flyer on the restroom door. Apparently, Mr. Shickles was coming later on in the week. Median had no intention of being here for that. Clowns were the shit icing on this shit cake.

The clown's eyes on the flyer followed him around too. And not in that general way, like with a painting. They moved randomly around in the clown's face.

Since he was wide awake and his bladder was full, he figured he may as well get up and go to the restroom. Median swung his legs out of the bed, and no sooner had his feet touched the floor than he heard someone in there.

"Oh!" a woman cried on the other side of the door.

Median held still, hyperalert.

"Please, stop!" the woman said. "No!"

He took a step closer and paused.

"Yes. Ooo, right there, yes! Oh, you're hurting me!"

He had more than a vague idea what was going on in there but was still confused. Median decided to intervene—it wasn't expressly "yes," so to him, that meant no. He pulled open the door and saw a Hispanic nurse with her skirt up over her hips. She had a mop handle gripped in one hand, and she blinked in surprise at him.

"A little privacy, please!" She kicked the door closed.

"Uh, excuse me," he said as the door shut in his face. "I have to pee, though," was what he had wanted to say, but somehow, the moment had passed.

Median shuffled back to his bed and sat while the nurse began moaning and…crying in anguish.

He looked over his shoulder at the other side of the room. The old man must have been checked out. A light breeze blew in the room from the open window, the chill going down his spine, and he found himself clenching.

Median didn't want to leave his room, so he shuffled about, searching for options. He found a jug on the opposite side of the other bed and hesitantly picked it up. It was weighty, and he gave it a shake, just to be sure. Liquid splished around inside, and he took it to the window, carefully unscrewing the top and holding it as far away from him as he could.

He opened the window, stuck his arm over the windowsill, and turned the container over. The urine glugged out, and he caught the quickest sniff of ammonia before shaking it one good time.

"Omigod! Is this urine?" someone shouted.

Median ducked, his nerves on end.

"It definitely smells like it, but wait. Let me taste it. It *is* urine! Oh god, why? Wait. Once more to be absolutely certain. Yes, that is *definitely* urine. And all over my nice new white shirt and matching white pants! Is this my own personal hell for all those people I urinated on?"

Crouching added pressure to his bladder, reminding him he needed to relieve himself. Median backed away from the window, pretty certain the besoiled person down there couldn't see him, then got on his knees. He shuffled around in his hospital gown until he could aim into the container.

"Why would somebody do this?" came the voice however many floors down. "How could hell possibly get worse? I'm in hell in hell! Double hell! Why? Whyyyy?"

Hell? Median thought.

Chapter 1 - No Clean Getaway

"My name Clean," the man in the wheelchair said.

Median was finishing off a Red Rocket Pop—a vaguely spaceship-shaped popsicle he'd enjoyed as a child. The man sitting next to him was long and lean, his skin dark as night. He was swathed in a ratty-looking brown robe, his snake-like head bald, like he'd never grown hair in his life.

Median didn't think Clean looked like he needed a wheelchair, but then again, Median didn't need one either. Nothing in St. Eloise Hospital was what it appeared to be when he really thought about it. He sucked the red juice off the wooden stick in his hand, aware the man was staring at him intently.

"You ever had yo ass washed?" Clean asked Median.

Median narrowed his gaze. Clean was giving him more eye than he could remember ever having received from anyone in his life. Median had an idea what the man was asking, considering he had worked part-time in the adult film industry for a few years.

"I have a nurse. She makes sure all of me gets clean." He smiled, hoping that would disarm Clean.

The man smiled back, his teeth a stark contrast of white against his blue-black skin. "Nah. I don't mean no regular bath." He leaned closer. "I mean, have somebody washed all up in your ass?" Then he made a show of letting his tongue dip and curl out of his mouth. It touched the point of his chin, then wound to the tip of his beak-like nose before he waved it up and down, like a paintbrush lapping a wall.

Median had been able to avoid being in guy-on-guy scenes, but he had been on the other side of the camera for a few dozen. Something about the man's expression—like he was reliving the last time he'd given an "ass-washing" and it had been akin to manna—unsettled Median. He had to admit to at least the slightest bit of intrigue.

"No-no, I can't say that I have had my salad tossed," he finally managed to say.

Clean shook his head again, his rheumy eyes going distant. "I don't mean no salad toss." He laid a hand over Median's. "You missin' out. I can send you to heaven."

"Aaaaand that's enough of that," Vinny said, suddenly pushing the wheelchair again.

Median didn't look back at the man. He had a flash of a waking nightmare where Clean's tongue lengthened and followed them down the hall.

"You got the stuff?" Median asked.

"Yup." Vinny shook the bag, and they headed straight for the elevator. "Dummy up. Nurse Tropos is always on the lookout."

"Right." Median did his best to let his face go slack. He'd been drugged before, but he didn't know how to *look* drugged.

A six-five, hawkish white woman in a nurse's uniform was scouring over everyone from a corner of the room. Median would have guessed there was a near equal number of staff and patients milling about. Unless she was looking for something specific, he didn't see how she'd make out much of anything he was or wasn't doing.

A massive *thing* Median could only describe as a sheet ghost stood next to the elevator doors. There was only the one elevator, which was odd for as much foot traffic as there was. The sheer size of this room dictated there should have been a bank of elevators, in Median's estimation.

The "ghost" had two eyeholes with two human-looking eyes staring through them. He would have guessed it was a bed sheet draped over a bodybuilder's bulky frame, except there were no legs sticking out the bottom. Median didn't know how to process that, but then again, some of the things he'd seen before coming here had been far stranger.

"How may I help you?" the ghost asked in a pleasant alto, doing something beneath the sheet that might or might not have been the folding of massive arms.

"My man!" There was a smile in Vinny's voice. "It's not what you can do for *me*; it's what *I* can do for you!" The paper bag rumpled, and a moment later, Vinny was standing next to the ghost, holding something low in his hand. Vinny looked around, checking to see if the coast was clear, and prodded him with it.

The ghost looked down, the hollow ovals of his eyes seeming to go wider.

"Is that a—"

"You know it, baby."

"Wha-what do you want for it?"

"Don't do nothin'," Vinny said, sliding the candy bar to him. "Just let me and my man walk on by."

The ghost looked around, taking the candy bar and running it beneath where Median guessed his nose was. He nodded.

"Aight, I feel you. But this is only good for a one-way trip."

Vinny held the bag up and shook it— obviously much more than one candy bar inside. Again, the eye holes in the ghost's bedsheet seemed to widen. The ghost thumbed the up button for the elevator.

Vinny smirked and pushed Median's wheelchair inside when the doors slid open.

"Well, that was easy." Median's heart hammered as they turned around.

"Good plans always start off easy," Vinny said. "Bad ones too." He stepped forward and pressed a button.

Median didn't recognize any of the symbols and was reminded of the time he had heard that you can't read in a dream.

But he was in hell. He wasn't dreaming. Right?

Chapter 2. *Mrs.* **Manhorn**

Mary stroked her belly, imagining the little life growing inside. She wasn't showing yet, and the pregnancy test she had taken indicated she wasn't pregnant, but she knew.

Mary was going to have a baby.

And all it had cost her was her husband's eternal soul.

It couldn't have been worth all that much, but it was all Rick had said he'd wanted. She had thought her hopes were dashed when her part in keeping Walker's pregnancy was revealed. She'd cared enough about her husband to not let him die, but Rick had come to her after the incident at the gymnasium with a new proposal. Not only was he *not* going to take her soul for betraying him, but he was still going to give her what she wanted.

A baby.

All she'd had to do was take Walker to St. Eloise.

The doorbell rang, and she sat up from Derek's large, warm body. He looked at her with those big, doe-brown eyes. Derek was so beautiful. The most beautiful man she'd ever met. Big and dumb, bless his heart. Before Median, she couldn't have imagined being with someone so empty-headed. So devoid of anything that could be described as desire. But the man who had swept her off her feet more than ten years ago had been so full of ideas, so *sharp,* but all his ideas had turned to shit.

She smiled at her fiancé, and he smiled back. Derek didn't talk much. He didn't think much either. The man just went to work, worked out at the gym, and came home to her. Well, he didn't work now because he'd had a work injury.

The fact he pounded her like Foreman on Frazier didn't hurt either. Well, sometimes it did, but only when Mary was in the mood for pain. Making love to Median had always been fun, adventurous, but Derek was a study in pressing every button inside her until she erupted. Sometimes, Mary thought she might suffer a concussion from her brain slamming into her skull like a battering ram.

Her fiancé didn't say anything when she stood, simply grinning. A smile seemed always safest for him. He didn't know he couldn't say the wrong thing with her. The fact he wasn't Walker M. Harris was enough.

It wasn't like her "husband"—if she technically had to call him that—was doing anything with what was left of his soul. He did porn, for chrissake. Sure, by the time he'd started, they were done with one another. After she'd lost her pregnancy, she just couldn't look at him the same anymore. She couldn't stand those puppy dog eyes looking at her.

Mary'd had to hate him to survive. Like tearing a life vest out of someone else's hands in the middle of a white squall so she wouldn't be the one to drown.

Walker had probably gone through his own thing too, but she'd had no capacity to take on

9

anyone else's grief after she'd been so *wounded.*
Mary had been orphaned by the time she met
Walker, and he had worked so hard to build a
bridge between his parents and her. His own
relationship with his father had been rocky prior to
the old man's stroke. They had eventually started
referring to her as their daughter, but the reality of
Martha's only child marrying a white woman had
been exacerbated by the fact that same white
woman hadn't been able to deliver her a
grandchild.

The loss had been threefold for Mary, and it
had taken years before she could see him as
anything other than the man who had…*infected* her
with cancerous hope. To have had her surrogate
family stripped away because of a womb that
couldn't grant her deepest desire.

The fact her body had rebelled against her,
while Walker had been unchanged physically or
emotionally, had also made it difficult for Mary to
look at him without a creeping sense of rage. The
miscarriage hadn't been his fault, but she couldn't
help reinterpreting his calm inexpressiveness as him
not giving a damn after she'd nearly bled to death.

Mary felt like she'd been stolen from but
had gradually been able to pack away the constantly
quiet anger baking inside her. She'd had to put on a
façade to be able to not only tolerate the world, but
also the presence of a man who was still her
husband on paper but not in her heart. He'd told her
about being in an adult film, had asked her what she
thought, like she was supposed to fling herself back
into his arms to stop him. Mary had very nearly

laughed in his face when she'd seen the ache in his eyes, but it hadn't been there when she'd lost the life inside her. Instead, she'd kept her mask from slipping.

Mary had had no choice but to accept she could never give birth. She and Walker were done, and she had forced herself to be content with the fact she'd never be a mother.

Until satan had come along.

His offer had been simple.

A child. A perfectly healthy baby born from her own womb.

She had immediately tossed aside all notion of contentment and supreme knowledge of the divine feminine—she'd reduced herself to nothing more than a haggard beggar, grasping onto the hem of his garment, after he'd approached her in that secret dark and offered—

Mary wrapped the robe around herself, smiling back at Derek and kissing him—the truest love of her life.

"You still want that baby?" the devil had asked.

The first time she'd betrayed Walker, she'd been shamed and had come to her senses, fighting alongside him once she realized she *did* care about him still. But the desire had raged anew when satan had returned with a second offer.

All she had to do was deliver him to St. Eloise Hospital and she could still have her child.

Mary sauntered out of their downstairs bedroom, through the kitchen—where she plucked a half stalk of celery out of a bowl on the island—and walked through the great room to the front door. Her heart skipped when she saw the shadowed outline of the person on the other side of the curtain.

"Good afternoon, Mrs. Harris," Mrs. Manhorn said when Mary approached the door.

There was no way the woman could have seen her inside, but she *knew*. What the old woman symbolized was terrifying enough, but Mary's fear had been exponentially raised after meeting her yesterday.

The peace she'd felt in Derek's arms just moments before was gone, shredded before the presence of this woman. Come to think of it, Mrs. Manhorn might *not* actually have been human.

She was an agent of Dr. Rick, which meant she could be any manner of being from human to devil…and her striking appearance—tall, angular frame, unfeminine save for a stripe of lipstick across lips as thin as a papercut, and mousy thin hair like god—or the devil—had slapped it on her head as an afterthought.

"Miss Manhorn!" Mary pulled the door open and forced a smile into her voice.

"It's *Mrs*. Manhorn," the woman said, her eyes darting around inside the house. "I am a married woman."

Mary stood back for her to come in, but the woman didn't move.

"Please. Come in."

Mrs. Manhorn raised a bony leg, and not for the first time, it reminded Mary of a poorly coordinated puppet, like the woman wasn't operating under her own power. She swayed for just

12

a moment before hauling the rest of her frail frame into the house.

Mrs. Manhorn made a straight line for the island in the kitchen. Mary hustled to catch up and was just in time to see the woman's look of disdain cast upon the bowl of vegetables Mary'd left.

She quickly crunched the bite of celery in her mouth and asked, "Could I get you anything to drink?" Mary pitched the rest of the celery she was holding in the garbage.

Mrs. Manhorn put her hands to either side of Mary's belly, lightly touching her. She nodded as if she were actually examining something. "Mrs. Harris, would you like to know what you're having?"

Had the woman been a real nurse, had she not been an underworldly agent, Mary would have understood the question and not mistaken its meaning.

"I-I…" Panic crawled up her throat. "No." The potential answer gave her thousands of pinpricks of terror in her—of all places—stomach.

The red smile scrawled across Mrs. Manhorn's face was as natural as a polar bear breakdancing on an airplane at fifty thousand feet. Mary didn't want to know the gender of the child she was having and hoped Mrs. Manhorn wasn't implying she might *not* be having a human being.

"Of course. Have you prepared for a home birth, or will you be going to the hospital?"

"Oh. Hospital. Definitely."

The thin woman nodded. "Have you thought about how you are going to explain?"

13

"Explain what?"

Mrs. Manhorn's eyes flicked down, then back up to somewhere on Mary's forehead. "The baby you're going to have."

Mary laughed nervously. "Well, they're doctors and nurses. I'm pretty sure they know."

Mrs. Manhorn shook her head. Left. Right.

"I mean, how will you explain having a child so *fast*."

Mary leapt over the first question that popped in her mind for the more pressing one. "How *fast*?"

"Three days."

"Three—" Mary covered her mouth. "But I'm not even showing."

"Three days, Mrs. Harris." Mrs. Manhorn picked up the bag she'd brought with her but never opened it. "I'll be back this time tomorrow and the day after to help you deliver. In case you change your mind about the hospital delivery."

"But wouldn't three days be the day *after* that?"

"Today is the first day."

Mary followed Mrs. Manhorn to the door like a pup at its master's heels, stepping around the woman to open the door for her.

"But I have to get so much stuff for the baby," Mary said. "We don't even have a crib."

Mrs. Manhorn smiled again, standing on the doorstep. This time, she looked much more human while she did it. "It sounds like you have a good problem on your hands. Goodbye, Mrs. Harris. See you tomorrow."

14

a lowercase hell

The woman stood on her doorstep longer than was courteous, and finally, Mary shut the door. No sooner had she turned away and was heading back to Derek when she felt a tremendous cramp in her bowels, doubling her over. Everything turned red with white at the corners, her pulse flaring in her vision. When she could see normally again, she was on her knees and her robe had fallen open, exposing her breasts and...

The tiniest paunch about the size of a cereal bowl.

Chapter 3. Motherfuckers

"Alfie," the angel said, holding a hand out to him.

Alfred had never been called that in his life, and he hated it instantly. But he was still disoriented, the instantaneous travel from the earthly plane to this…place having had a jarring effect on him.

"Is this…heaven?"

Instead of answering, the man, who had been leaning over, stood and stretched his arms to the sky. A massive pair of wings extended from his back, easily stretching ten feet to either side of him.

"He" was golden-skinned, with long, flowing hair hanging about his shoulders in bronze ringlets. The angel was bare-chested, wearing only a white sarong. He pulled his powerful arms from the sky as if they had been holding up the ceiling of the world.

"I'm bored," the angel said, seemingly to no one in particular.

Alfred pulled himself out of a hole in the earth, expecting his body to be stiff or sore. But he rose with ease, feeling the strength he had always known surging through him. Whether this was heaven or hell, he saw no cause not to pick up where he'd left off when he'd been alive.

He seized the "angel" by the throat and squeezed. The flesh was pliant. Alfred even felt the strong throb of a pulse beneath his thumb.

But despite Alfred's tight grip on thick, ropey muscle, the angel merely turned his head and looked at him, his wings slowly folding back into place. "Kochab, what else is there interesting to see around here?" he asked.

"Wait," another voice behind him said. "This might be good."

Alfred felt vulnerable. He hadn't even bothered to look around to see who else was here. Though he was open to attack, he didn't dare take his eyes off this one to assess his surroundings.

The angel Alfred was attempting to strangle sighed his impatience and rolled his eyes. He looked at Alfred, staring at him, expecting him to do *something*.

"No." He slapped Alfred's hand away as if it were a buzzing fly and began strolling away from him. "Let us go see the other one. The one who speaks oddly."

"They *all* speak oddly," Kochab said.

"Yes, but he uses words in a particularly strange manner, I hear."

Alfred's hand stung where the angel had hit it, and he rubbed it subconsciously, finally looking around. Rolling green hills were as far as he could see, the sky a clean blue. Everything appeared the same in every direction, and he couldn't even tell one point from another. There wasn't even a sun.

He glanced down at the hole he'd climbed out of. It was oblong, almost egg-shaped, maybe three feet deep and big enough for him to fit in with his legs curled up.

"Is that how people get here?" he asked.

Alfred looked at the angels slowly walking away from him. They held hands and laughed with one another. Other than the two of them and the hole he'd emerged from, everything Alfred could see looked the same.

He followed them.

Alfred was more curious than afraid. The angel he'd tried to strangle had an easy strength far surpassing his, and he guessed Kochab—slightly shorter but with blond hair and even broader shoulders—was likely just as powerful.

He immediately hated the both of them. They had power beyond his. And as they were agents of heaven—if that indeed was this place— Alfred hated it too and whomever had created it.

They were both several inches taller than him, and their leisurely long-legged pace was a labor for him to keep up with.

The smaller hills were part of a larger slope they were cresting. Alfred followed, first spotting the grand oblong spires of a strange city in the distance, the greatest of all piercing the sky and beyond. They were long and twisted, with bits of green placed randomly on them. Alfred looked harder, realizing these were trees. He thought the angels were going there until they turned onto a path which seemed to lead away from the city.

It was winding and pointless, and Alfred was certain whoever had made the path was an idiot. Probably a procession of idiots who had worn the path simply by walking no place in particular. He should have just abandoned following these two and gone to the city. It was the only thing that had any potential so far. But if this were heaven, could he do bad here?

The angels came to an open space at the end of the path. They were still holding hands and staring at something he couldn't see. Curiosity got the better of Alfred, and he walked right up to them, breaking their grasp when he stepped farther into the clearing.

There was another oblong hole, like the one he'd come out of, with a boulder about the size of three men a few feet away.

"Come out, come out," the one not Kochab said.

"You get him," Kochab said to Alfred. "He is shy."

Alfred was curious enough to not take offense at being ordered. He walked quietly, nervous for the first time he could ever remember.

It was a man, and he was filthy, like he'd dug himself out of that hole. Or maybe like he'd tried digging deeper *into* it. Alfred had noticed several small mounds of dirt outside the hole when he'd passed.

The man had crazy eyes, and yet they were familiar. Alfred had just begun to ponder when the man looked up at him, nervously chewing on the neck of his soiled shirt. He smiled.

"Angel?" Hammercock asked.

"Shit," Alfred said.

Chapter 4. A Flaccid Penis Smearing Across the Window

"Be careful who you talk to," Vinny said when they came off the elevator. He handed Median another Red Rocket Pop. "Suicides."

"What, they might try to convince me to kill myself?" Median unwrapped it and took a chomp off the top, chewing it too fast and giving himself brain freeze.

"No, they'll talk your ear off. You'd think people who did themselves in would be the ones who had everything wrapped up before they went. If I had a dime for every time somebody told me they wished they'd let the dog out…"

"Yeah. I guess they probably died too."

"No. Their beloved Spot started eating them after the dog chow ran out."

Median grimaced. "That's not true, is it? Dogs don't really eat their owners after they die." Median hoped it wasn't true, at least. He'd never had a pet before.

"Sure, it is. Cats are even worse. Sometimes they don't even wait until they run out of food. The second you die, they see you as meat. Eat your pop."

They passed another nurse who looked just like the one downstairs. Median joyfully ate his popsicle, even enjoying the idea it made him look simple to any staff bothering to pay attention.

"Why do I need to be in this wheelchair again?" He asked between lipsmacks. "I can walk."

"Because. It's St. Elo policy. This might be hell, but even we have insurance liabilities."

"Let me guess—lawyers?"

"*Haha*, yeah. But despite your thinking, lawyers don't automatically come down here. People hate 'em because they think of the bad stuff typically before everybody else. And either they write rules to safeguard you or they take advantage of a situation that could have been prevented."

Vinny wheeled him to what seemed like the middle of the room and stopped.

"What's up?" Median asked.

"I don't know. This is where I thought you'd do your magic."

"My magic?" Median deep-throated the stick to get the last chunk of popsicle from the base. Vinny wiggled his eyebrows, and Median gave the demon the finger. "How am I supposed to know who it is?"

"How am *I* supposed to know?" Median handed Vinny the stick, and he tossed it over his shoulder. "I'm just an enterprisin' demon lookin' to get the hell out of hell. You're…y'know…*human*. Do some human shit or somethin'. It's not like this place is Fort Knox. Chosen-one that shit."

Median looked around the room. Half the people he saw were having conversations; half were alone or otherwise occupied with their thoughts. He didn't see anything about any of them that stuck out or gave him the impression they were particularly special.

Median continued scanning the room, no one catching his eye.

"Okay, I gotta go see a guy," Vinny said. "You good here for a minute?"

"Yeah." Median nodded, and the demon walked away, heading out of the room and into the hall. He looked around. The one nurse in this ward had disappeared, and he figured it was safe to move, although he didn't dare get out of his wheelchair.

Median rolled over to a corkboard tacked with notices and flyers. There was a motorcycle for sale, a condo for rent, and someone selling Girl Scout Cookies. What the hell was this? It all seemed so...*normal.* There was a crumpled piece of paper with a hand drawing—a ragged-looking figure, fist raised, and the words "Join the Rebellion" printed above it. Vinny had said he'd given him the abbreviated version of how St. Elo worked, but Median was going to need some extra clarification.

Apparently, the insurance adjusters weren't too worried about patients and staff getting hurt, though. Every piece of paper up there was pinned with a thumbtack, and if a person were motivated enough, they could do some damage.

Median spotted a bifold card mostly obscured by flyers. He reached for it, but it was too high for him from his chair. Median looked around. Everyone seemed to be otherwise preoccupied, and that nurse hadn't come back.

He could do this quick, he thought, rising from the chair and reaching for the card.

"You're that guy, aren't you?" someone asked. "*The* guy."

Icy splinters of panic lanced his stomach. Median had the corner of the card pinched between

22

index and middle fingers but didn't have enough grasp to pull it down. He sat hard, pain shooting up into his guts, and was pretty sure he'd just sat on one of his balls.

"'Scuse me?" Median said. *Damn*. He'd opened his mouth. Should have just sat back and drooled on himself again.

"The one they brought in here—" the man began to say before a woman with a massive head of salt and pepper hair elbowed him when she walked past. "The one they brought in here the other day."

Median mentally kicked himself and looked at the man. He was disheveled, his receding hair long and wily about his head. The man looked about mid-fifties, with large dark semi-circles beneath his black eyes and milk-pale skin.

"I'm...I'm Median," Median said.

The man cracked an open-mouthed smile, but Median couldn't see any teeth. "I'm Martin. I killed myself."

"Oh?" Median tried to feign more interest than he really felt. There was a conversation coming, and Median saw no way around It. He was going to have to grin and bear it. "Sorry about that?" He offered his hand to shake, and the man looked down at it like he didn't recognize what it was.

"So, you're going to sneak out of here?"

"'Scuse me?" Median had no clue how the man could have known about the plan.

"Yeah. I heard you're going to break out. When are you gonna do it? Before or after the upheaval?"

"The up*what*al?" Median stared at him.

"Oh, I'm not gonna tell anybody. Besides, who's listening to any of us?" The man gestured to everyone else in the room. "I'm probably going to join the rebellion."

Median had no idea what he was talking about and felt like he had to change the subject. "Um, why'd you kill yourself?"

Something faded from the man's empty smile. "Gladys." His eyes went distant. "She was the love of my life." He shrugged. "Or something like that. I fell in *like* with her in high school, but you know teens. If you're in, you're in. If you're out, you're looking in. She was in; I was out. I was bold enough to ask her for her number one day, and surprise, surprise—she gave it to me. I was so scared, it took a week before I worked up the nerve to call.

"But I did, and she actually answered. We talked. God knows about what at this point. Typical fifteen-year-old stuff, I'd say. I remember I made her laugh." Martin's smile broadened. He *did* have teeth, and Median felt a measure of relief for some reason. "We talked a couple more times on the phone, hardly ever in school, but whenever I called, there was a fifty-fifty shot she'd actually pick up.

"Gradually, though, she stopped answering. I was lovesick, but I wasn't stupid. I got the hint. Life carried on. I met who I *thought* was my high school sweetheart, got married, had a career and kids, got divorced. On a whim, I looked that girl up. My pre-sweetheart. It had to have been almost thirty years since we'd last spoken, but when I called, she answered. And she *remembered* me!"

Median thought he gleaned the shine of a tear in the man's eye. Martin shook his head.

"We must have talked…for hours. I don't know what I was looking for…No, I know what I was looking for. She'd probably been the most beautiful girl in high school. You know what I was looking for."

Martin laughed.

"But I was prepared to say goodbye. I don't know. I'd…satisfied something inside me. I was okay if all there was was just that one phone call.

"But you know what? She invited me to come see her. She was only two cities away. All of a sudden, hope that I hadn't known in over thirty years leapt alive in me. I said I'd come tomorrow if she liked, and she told me in three days. She'd just had a procedure in the hospital and needed a little more time to heal.

"Let me tell you, those three days were the longest year of my life." Martin shook his head, and Median was doing all he could not to roll his eyes. "Finally, the day comes. I drive to her house, not too dressed up, but not too casual—my favorite pair of jeans and a new sport jacket with a polo shirt. A white woman greeted me at the door, showed me in. While I was still wondering who she was, the smell of antiseptic and…and *death* wafted through the air.

"The woman, who turned out to be her nurse, led me to a room at the back of the house, where I saw her hooked up to a half dozen machines doing just about every human function for her.

"'It's not contagious,' she said to me, after I had been standing there in shock long enough. I came closer, that death-antiseptic scent like a punch to my sense of smell. I wanted to run away, to not have any of my senses assaulted by what barely passed for a human being in front of me. But I'd asked for this. I'd been secretly asking for this for the last thirty-plus years.

"'Are you still in love with me?' she asked, and I laughed. I tried to make it one of those what-are-you-talking-about laughs, but it was more like she'd pulled the curtain back on my darkest secret. That I would have gladly turned my back on everything I'd done over the last three decades. That I would have eagerly reversed it all, just to be with this woman. Even then.

"'Yes,' I said. And I stood there like a man waiting to be judged. She looked away from me.

"'I should have been dead three months ago,' she said. 'I always wondered what was keeping me here.' Then she looked at me again.

"'Not you.' It was like a stab in the heart. All this time, I'd been pining away for her. There were times when she crossed my mind—the day I got married, when my first child was born, when I paid off the house. All things I hid away from myself, even. Things I would have wanted to do with *her*." Martin shook his head again. "All dust with those two words. And she kept saying them over and over again.

"'Not you. Not you. Not you.' She started laughing when she said it. Here I was, barely fifty years old—a fantastic career, beautiful children, an ex-wife who didn't completely hate me—laid down on the altar before the first and only person I probably had ever truly loved, and she was carving my guts out with a smile on her face.

"I ran away from everything. Stopped going to my job, stopped taking phone calls from my kids. Everything reminded me of her. Because now I had no illusion about everything I did. I'd always wanted it to be her. The mother of my children, my partner as I advanced in my career, someone to tour the world and grow old with...I think I thought it would have been okay the way it all happened, so long as I eventually got to have her. I would have even taken her on her deathbed. But even then, shriveled up and at death's door, she rejected me." Martin scratched at his temple. "That's how I wound up here."

Damn, Vinny was right. Suicides would *try to talk your ear off.*

"That's nice," Median said, not knowing what to say exactly. "I mean, sad. Very sad. Oh my lord—what the hell is that?"

Median almost leapt out of his wheelchair at the sight of what looked like a giant pink rag. It slapped against one of the large windows on the other side of the room and slowly began dragging across.

"Oh, that's just the window wiper," Martin said, only glancing over his shoulder.

Median was captivated while the "rag" strafed, the top clearly spreading to look like an eyeless face complete with eyebrows and a beard. His eyes drifted down, and yes, that was definitely a flaccid penis smearing across the window.

Several more skins slapped against the remaining three windows: one a woman's, by what appeared to be a pair of large-areolaed breasts crushed against the glass; a second man's, by the sheer volume of body hair; and a fourth Median couldn't tell the gender of because it appeared to have been slapped against the window backfirst, but it did have beautiful tresses of long blond hair.

The skins were held by impossibly long, black and gray, squid-like tentacles using the floppy arms and legs like handles while they cleaned.

"So, what brings you down here?" Martin asked, putting a hand on his shoulder to keep Median from rolling away.

"Look," Median said, glancing around, "I'm looking for someone. I don't know who but somebody who holds part of a key to me getting out of here."

Martin's eyebrows went up.

"I have to be gone in less than three days."

"Three days, huh?" Martin asked. "So you're going to miss the wedding? We're gonna fight."

"Fight? Wedding? What wedding? What fight?" Median wasn't sure, but he thought Martin was conflating the two.

"Dr. Rick's getting married. To one of the nurses."

"One of the nurses?" The words just came out of Median's mouth. The devil's name being spoken gave him goose-chills. He wasn't really aware of what he was saying. "To who?"

Martin snapped his fingers several times, trying to conjure the name from his memory. He finally looked over his shoulder at two patients talking animatedly behind him. "Hey guys, who's Dr. Rick marrying again? Which one of the nurses?"

Median's initial feeling was he really didn't care, but suddenly he did. What kind of person—*or demon*—would intentionally marry the devil? Or did she even know who he was? Martin was sitting on the back of a ratty couch. He stood and stepped past Median.

"Let me get that."

Martin reached toward the corkboard, fished beneath papers, grabbed the bifold card, and yanked it down. He turned it over, his eyes scanning the outside, then he opened it.

"Yeah. Beatricia." Martin nodded.

The name sent chills down Median's spine. The devil had had a trick up his sleeve after all. No boyfriend, no husband, but a fiancé. And *he* was the fiancé. Median didn't know any of the staff except for Nurse Tropos and Vinny.

"Ohhhhh, her," said a rail-thin Asian man with salt and pepper facial hair. He was as bald as a bowling ball otherwise. The man held up his hands in front of his chest to signify big breasts.

"No, not her, you idiot," said a chubby white woman with tears in her eyes. "The skinny one with

29

the pouty lips. The blond one?" She pointed to the blond skin scrubbing the corner of one of the windows like it was her.

"Ohhhhh." The Asian man nodded. "Who?"

Wait—hadn't Median held up his end of the deal? He couldn't exactly remember. Median had given birth, but where was the baby? Broken pieces of memories came back to him. He couldn't remember holding the baby or even what the baby had looked like. But he knew for certain *he* didn't have it, so didn't that mean Rick did?

So that meant he'd done his part. They'd agreed he'd get to meet her. Median didn't want to force her into anything. He'd resigned himself to the possibility she would just get up and walk out after they'd had lunch, but he was hopeful. Median wanted to hear her voice…to look into her eyes. But learning Rick was *engaged* to her felt like Median had been cheated.

The fact they hadn't agreed where the two would meet made her being down here sensible to him too. They probably would wind up in the cafeteria to fulfill the bargain, and then he'd be shipped off to hell proper, while *she married the fucking devil*.

Median vowed this shit would not stand. He had to get vengeance if it was literally his last act. Revenge against the devil whilst in hell or hell adjacent didn't really seem like a possible thing, but if Median had ever prayed for anything, he prayed for retribution.

"Buddy, you okay?" Martin asked, pulling Median out of his own thoughts. He chuckled. "You look like you just saw a ghost."

"No." Median shook his head. "I think I just got screwed by the devil. Impregnated first. Then screwed."

The man made a face, like what Median had said made sense.

If he were here…and she were here…and if the devil kept his word she would have lunch with him…there might be a way.

"You look like you just saw another ghost."

Median forced himself to laugh. "I'm all right." The idea had begun to form in his head. He continued looking at that one last skin.

It was really zeroing in on a spot. Something about it was familiar.

How do you fuck with the king of fucking with people? Rick had seemed to have an ego, like anyone else. Maybe just larger than most. And then Median knew—he was going to break up the wedding.

And then he realized—that skin with a fuzz of blond, currently doing circles on the fourth window, was Vinny's.

"Aw shit," Median said.

Chapter 5. Babies and Murder

In a lot of ways, Mary considered herself lucky. She'd fallen in love twice with men who worshipped her. That was figurative in Derek's case, but it had been very literal with Walker. It wasn't often a man pledged his eternal soul to a woman. She recalled him getting on his knees in the Checkers parking lot all those years ago. That had made an impression on her when she'd been on the verge of dumping him. She reflected on the spectacular failure of their marriage but didn't consider their time together a bad thing.

Without Walker, she wouldn't have met Derek. And without Derek, she wouldn't have met the devil. And without the devil, she wouldn't be in Tops 'n Tots, shopping for a baby who apparently was coming in just a few days.

Derek pushed the cart, patient as ever while Mary went up and down every aisle, examining just about everything on the shelves, including items she had no intention of buying, like Similac. Mary was going to breastfeed.

Wait, was she?

What if she wasn't able to? What if her baby would need something other than breastmilk? What if it took something more…substantial to feed her child? Oh god, what if her baby had *teeth*?

"You know, I think I'm going to get a few of these, just in case," she said to Derek. "Don't you think?"

He looked at her with those large hazel puppy dog eyes and shrugged. Her man was always supportive. Mary couldn't recall a single time he'd ever told her no.

A year ago, Derek had been on the second floor of a house on fire when the floor had given way, and he'd fallen two stories into the basement. He'd broken his back and both legs and still managed to come out, shielding a puppy with his body as he crawled.

Derek seemed as healthy as ever now—six and a half feet of brick-hard muscle—but still hadn't been cleared to go back to work. Even though Derek was quiet and introspective, there was something about him that didn't seem real. Maybe because he was too physically perfect. Despite being manly, he was also the most beautiful man Mary had ever seen.

She'd thought Median had been pretty when they first met, but Derek's soft chocolate skin, the constant shadow of a beard, even though he shaved daily, honey-brown eyes that always seemed to be looking off in the distance, well-deep dimples, and high cheekbones made him model-esque, on par with Tyson Beckford or any major male movie star who graced screens for no other reason than being eye candy.

Derek probably could have had just about any woman he wanted. Women flirted with him openly right in front of her. But he either had the grace to not embarrass them with a passive rejection or he didn't notice them at all. He was all hers.

"I gotta pee," Mary said. "Could you meet me over by the cribs?"

He smiled, his thick lips revealing perfect, rectangular teeth. Derek wrapped her up with his massive arms, squeezing just enough to make her want to stay there. She breathed in the musky-sweet scent that almost smelled like food.

"I'll count the moments until I see you there."

Mary's belly had only gotten bigger over the last few hours, her budding baby pressing on her bladder. Derek hadn't even questioned her rapidly changing body. It was like nothing bad about her mattered, so long as he got to have her.

By the time she neared the women's room, she was almost running, the urge to pee like a dam on the verge of breaking. Mary was thankful she'd worn a skirt, quickly hiking it and sliding her underwear down after she'd latched the stall door. She hovered over the toilet, and before she went, someone shoved the outer door open, apparently in as much a rush to go as she was. The woman took the stall next to hers and latched the door.

Mary had finished her business and flushed the toilet without hearing anything from next door. She came out and went to the sink. Though she wasn't trying to look, she couldn't help but see the woman's shoes to either side of the toilet, like she was straddling it.

And then the torrent came.

It came out of the woman like a racehorse, and Mary paused at the sink without turning the water on, amazed. She'd never heard anything like that come out of a human before and watched the woman's feet in awe as it went on and on.

Mary thought she'd been half mesmerized, losing track of exactly how long the woman went on peeing. Finally, it slowed to a half dozen healthy trickles that had to have splashed the woman's inner thighs. Mary wondered how close the bowl was to overflowing.

Finally, the woman flushed and opened the door. Mary averted her eyes, preoccupying herself with turning on the sink, and pumped two squirts of liquid soap into her palm.

"Mrs. Walker," the woman said.

Mary looked up at the reflection. It was her nurse.

"Mrs. Manhorn! So strange to see you here. Small world."

"I do not consider a population of eight billion, two hundred two thousand, thirty-three small."

"It's just an expression."

Mrs. Manhorn approached the sinks, but rather than turning one on, she began adjusting the single bun on top of her head. Mary tried her best to not make a face of disgust. The woman fixed her with an expression both blank and sharp at the same time, giving the bun one last squeeze, as if commanding it to stay put.

"I see you are coming along expediently."

"Uh." Mary turned off the water once her hands had been thoroughly rinsed. "Oh, yeah. My fiancé and I are getting some things for the baby."

"Mrs. Walker, I am not one to judge. Your life is your business, so long as you maintain certain agreements."

Mary thought she heard a little extra stress put on "Mrs." Certainly, a woman in the employment of the devil didn't think she had a right to judge Mary for getting engaged before she was divorced. And then it hit her.

Mary would never *be* divorced.

She was going to be a widow.

Walker was going to die. In hell.

"You know, Mrs. Manhorn, what if I *did* want to change my mind?"

The older woman turned her head, then her eyes followed, swiveling in her skull until they locked onto Mary. She dropped her arms.

"Mrs. Walker. You have made an agreement with my employer. If you were to renege on said agreement, then I would be forced to remove that bundle of joy from your...custody."

Mary took a step back from the woman.

"You aren't changing your mind, are you, *Mrs.* Walker?" Mrs. Manhorn took a step closer.

"No. I...was just asking a question."

Mrs. Manhorn reached for her, and Mary's back was suddenly against the door. The woman placed her unclean hands atop Mary's swollen belly, and she smiled, the wrinkled skin around her eyes like hanging curtains, ready to drop at any moment.

"Good."

Mary got a good look at the woman's teeth and thought they didn't belong in a human mouth. They were dark yellow and had lines like cracks throughout, like they would shatter if she bit into anything denser than an apple. Mrs. Manhorn pressed down hard.

"Because I would hate to reach inside you and tear out the growing little life you prayed so hard for that you tied the soul of your true love to the Infernal One. Sewer of Discord, the Son of All, and Plucker of the Fruit."

Mary didn't know all those names, but she was pretty certain who the woman was talking about. And her hand against Mary's belly was starting to hurt.

"Let…go of me!"

Mrs. Manhorn stopped moving. The older woman's arm had stiffened, and Mary grabbed her wrist, trying to pry her hand away.

"Please…Mrs. Manhorn. Stop!" She didn't want to hurt the woman, but her survival instinct wouldn't let her just stand there. Mary balled her open hand into a tight fist and threw a swift left hook, connecting on the point of the older woman's chin.

"Oo!" Mrs. Manhorn said, her eyes bouncing around in her head. She stumbled backward.

In her panic, Mary's adrenaline had been flowing, and she thought she might have hit Mrs. Manhorn much harder than intended. The nurse's arms pinwheeled, and she scrambled to keep her feet under her. Mary leaned forward, meaning to help her, but instead, she put her palm into the center of the woman's chest and shoved.

Mrs. Manhorn fell seemingly in slow motion, her eyes locking onto Mary's. There was a loud *crunch* when she hit the floor, her head perpendicular to her body where her neck and head had caught against the wall.

Those eyes were still homed onto Mary's—blame, hatred, and what Mary would have sworn was delight while the life drained out of them. She turned and fled the restroom, still feeling Mrs. Manhorn's gaze burrowing into her back.

Chapter 6. As You Wished

"I did as you asked, Angel," Hammercock said. The idiot had his hands out to Alfred in supplication, as if Alfred could bless him, even if he were inclined.

"Stand up, you buffoon," Alfred said to him.

Hammercock stood without the aching protests of his knees. Apparently, being dead could fix everything but stupid.

"Regale us," Penemue—as Alfred had learned his name was—said.

Hammercock looked at the real angel, then back to him.

"You really are…beautiful," he said before spotting Kochab behind Penemue.

"I told you he would not be as interesting as was foretold," Kochab said.

"Prove your love for me." Alfred felt something akin to jealousy at how Hammercock had looked at the angels. "Kill them."

The man looked doubtful for a moment, then nodded. Alfred was certain Hammercock had no hope against two such impressive physical specimens, but he would be free of the man at the very least.

Hammercock was tall, but next to the angels, he looked like a subspecies. Alfred thought about that for a moment. Perhaps humans were. Angels were supposedly the primary species, and mankind was an afterthought. God had become bored with them and wanted to delight in something new. But for angels and humans to look so similar,

39

to Alfred that meant They either thought the original design was still good enough to emulate or They were just incredibly lazy.

Alfred had to admit, the man was savvy. Hammercock had a "street sense" to him that made him approach most things in a very practical manner.

While the two angels conversed, he stepped behind them and picked up a stone bigger than his fist. Hammercock paused a moment, hefting it as if mentally measuring one of them, and then rushed Kochab, swinging high and catching the angel in the base of the skull.

The blow truly had taken the angel by surprise, and he fell to his knees. Penemue, instead of becoming alarmed, put his hands to his stomach and guffawed mightily. Hammercock turned on him and, with both hands, jammed as much of the stone into the angel's wide open mouth.

Penemue's eyes enlarged, and he stumbled backward, blue-green blood pouring from his mouth. Hammercock delivered a series of savage kicks to the crotch that either were ineffective or hurt nowhere near as much as his mouth.

Kochab stood and took a shaky step with a sandaled foot. Hammercock switched tactics and began kicking at Penemue's knees, finally sending him down to one. The angel still was covering his mouth with both hands, blood gushing between his fingers. Nose to nose, Hammercock began gouging one of the angel's eyes, twisting furiously with his thumb until Kochab was suddenly behind him—a

distance of at least a half dozen feet crossed in a
fraction of a second—and spun him around.

Penemue lowered his hands from his ruined
mouth and spat the stone out, along with blue-green
gore and chips of broken teeth. He and Kochab
seized Hammercock by an arm apiece, and they *tore*
him almost in half, down to his waist, and dropped
him where he stood.

"My teeth, Koko," Penemue said, spitting
again. A long blue-green trail of saliva stretched
from his lip.

"Oh, *Mue.* Let us see." Kochab stepped
closer to examine and poked two fingers in the
other angel's mouth, fishing out a shard of a broken
tooth. He placed it in a brooch on his hip and
cinched it closed, then used part of his own sash to
dab at Penemue's shredded lip. "Better?"

The other angel nodded, rolling his tongue
over his gums, and dammit if he didn't have two
perfect rows of teeth when he smacked his healed
lips and opened his mouth.

"Let's go see the first one again."

"Morgan?"

"Maybe *he'll* be some fun," one of them
said. They took wing and rose into the sky.

"At least they finally weren't boring."
Alfred watched them until they were dots over the
city.

"Angel!"

Alfred glanced where Hammercock's body
lay. His arm had been pulled away from his torso,
one long strip of flesh connecting the appendage to
his waist. They'd wishboned him. "You're alive?"

41

Alfred approached out of curiosity. There surprisingly wasn't a lot of blood, even though Hammercock appeared to be in a great amount of agony. His arm looked more like an accessory rather than an actual piece of him, and Alfred knelt, poking Hammercock's head with a finger. The man twitched, opening his tear-filled eyes and looking around until they settled on Alfred.

The old man seemed to relax somewhat but was definitely hurting.

"How are you still living?" Alfred asked, more to himself than to Hammercock.

"By your love…I'm sure of it." His voice was high and reedy. "Could you please take some of this pain away?"

Alfred thought a moment, shushing Hammercock when his groans of agony got too loud. Finally, he looked down at him and said, "If you truly believe in me, then I have already taken your pain away."

Hammercock was clearly struggling, doing his best to stifle his cries, Alfred continued watching his arm. The strip of flesh slowly zipped back up, like a…like a…

"Like a banana being peeled in reverse," Alfred said.

Hammercock had gone red in the face, when Alfred believed he had figured it out. The man had died. He was in heaven because he'd jumped out the window of a building and fallen to his death. Alfred didn't quite get how the man's suicide hadn't sent him straight to hell, but that was a debate for another time. Hammercock couldn't die now because he was already dead.

"I want to see something." Alfred grabbed Hammercock's wrist and pulled, retearing the newly knitted flesh.

Hammercock cried out, but then stifled himself, biting his lips to keep quiet. Alfred stood and turned toward the city, with its spiring trees. He stared for a long moment.

"So the dead can't die," he said, thinking of a new purpose for himself.

Alfred was going to find a way to murder. In heaven.

Chapter 7. Thomas T. Telford Is the Worst Person Who Ever Lived

"So, is anybody going to do anything about Vi—*that orderly guy*?" Median asked for the fifth time as he was pushed back to his room.

"I assure you, Mr. Walker," Nurse Tropos began, stopping in front of his bed, "everything is under control." She locked the wheel of his wheelchair before coming around to his side.

"I can—"

Median was about to tell her he could get out of his chair on his own when she scooped him up like a pile of dirty clothes and rested him gently on his bed. The woman was tall and thin and appeared to be somewhere in her late fifties, but she was so *strong*.

"Now you just rest here," she said. "Someone will be along to get you for your appointment with Dr. Saranc soon." Nurse Tropos examined his bandaged arm. "In the meantime, here's a popsicle." She presented it seemingly from nowhere and held it out.

"Dr. who?" Median took it and began unwrapping it almost subconsciously.

"No. Dr. Saranc. Dr. Hu is on Floor Seven." Nurse Tropos left the room before he could rephrase his question.

A moment later, another patient was wheeled into his room. It had to be his roomie from before, although Median had never seen the man. He and the nurse, a pretty redhead who was thin and even taller than Nurse Tropos, came in laughing.

"And so he says," the old man began, "'if I ever see you in here again, you sonofabitch, I'll kill you!'

"I says to him, I say, 'What's the sermon next week, Father?'"

He descended into brackish cackles, like he was making popcorn in his lungs. The tall nurse helped him into bed, red in the face herself.

Median raised his bed so he could get a better look. He couldn't recall if he'd seen the man earlier this morning when he'd left. But he remembered seeing him—at least a part of him—his first night here. The night he hoped had just been a nightmare.

If he prayed for anything ever, Median prayed he'd never see that *thing* in his dreams again.

The tall nurse gave the old man a peck on the cheek and a little finger wave when she left the room. Her actions had struck Median as deeply unprofessional, but what about this place wasn't? It was hell, afterall.

"So, new guy, what's your name?" the old man asked.

Median had been watching the nurse leave, eating his popsicle and then staring out into the hall. He slowly wound his attention back to the man in the other bed.

"Median," he said. "Median Harris."

"That's a weird name. I bet there's a weird story behind it."

Median laughed. "Yeah. Depends on which one of my parents you ask. My father grew up in a

45

little town in Ohio called Medina, and he wanted to name me that if I'd been a girl. He said my parents had an agreement that he'd get first name for a girl and she'd get first name for a boy. Out I came, and he still liked Medina, so he switched two letters and made 'Median' my middle name. My first name is actually Walker."

"And what's your mother's story?"

Median frowned while he recalled it. "She said it was a town too. But she wasn't from there. She was just passing through with her folks when she was a teenager. She said it had a profound effect on her. The odd part is, they both contradict each other's story. She said my father isn't from Medina. She said he's from Toledo."

"And he says?"

"That there's no such city as 'Median'."

"Spell your middle name?" the old man asked.

"M-E-D-I-A-N."

"Yeah. Not by that spelling."

"Hm?"

"My name's Thomas T. Telford."

The name immediately rang a bell for Median. "Hey, I know you…"

"I doubt it, son. I have a condition called prosopagnosia—I never forget a face."

Median nodded, not sure what to say to that.

"So what city did they bring you in from?"

"Um, Detroit?" Median wasn't exactly sure how to answer that question.

46

"No-no." Thomas T. Telford laughed. "I don't mean up there. I mean down *here*. What city were you in?"

"I don't understand. This is hell. What do you mean 'city'?"

Thomas T. Telford laughed again. "Son, what you just said is tantamount to saying to a Californian that you're from America. There's districts, cities, *governments* down here. They brought me in from M'th."

"Muh…Muh-what?"

"M'th. It's about a hundred fifty thousand paces west from Pandemonium."

Median shook his head. "Pandemonium?"

"Jesus, kid. That's the capital city of hell. How do you not know that? How long have you been down here?"

"Since yesterday."

"Yesterday? But you were *here* yesterday."

Median nodded, not sure what to say.

"Shit. So you really *are* fresh from the tap." Thomas T. Telford looked thoughtfully for a short moment.

"Are you alive?" he asked in a whisper.

"I don't think so," Median said. "I thought if you were down here that meant you're dead."

"Do you remember dying?"

"No."

"Shit, son. Dying should be something you should remember. You sure you were ever alive to begin with? Three of my ex-wives murdered me." Thomas T. Telford smiled, his eyes going distant.

"Is being murdered a…*good* memory for you?"

"The way they did it, it was." Thomas T. Telford's smile broadened. "I was a ripe shit in life. I made peace a long time ago that I was going to hell, and I made the trip worth it."

"So…how are you here?" Median asked. "I mean, as far as I understood, St. Eloise was supposed to be some sort of rehab so people could eventually be more effectively tormented by the sufferings of hell."

Thomas T. Telford opened his mouth to speak, then something went slack behind his eyes and he sat back in bed. His attention turned toward the window. Outside, what looked like a molten fireball in the middle of a giant mountain lit up the entire tortured landscape.

"Time for your therapy appointment, Mr. Walker," a man said, pushing in a wheelchair.

Median was about to explain how he was in the middle of a conversation he wanted to finish, but something about the lack of expression on Thomas T. Telford's face told him that was over.

Chapter 8. That Time Mary Doomed Her Husband to Hell

Mary was nervous. She'd accidentally killed her nurse, and now she was at her check-up. The expectant mother had no idea what they would say or if they'd even involve the authorities, but she was even more afraid *not* to show up.

Derek had wanted to come, but she'd convinced him this appointment was so mundane his time would be better spent assembling the baby's crib. She'd expected much more of a fuss, but he was so damned *agreeable*.

Mary parked the tiny Fiat rental she'd gotten after Median and Joe had totaled her car. She'd never been here before, had probably only visited the city of Inkster a handful of times. Mary sat and examined St. Eloise Hospital from the middle of the parking lot for a long time.

It was old and big and kind of looked like the Masonic Temple downtown. Mary exited her vehicle and pressed the lock button on her key fob twice, making the car chirp to signify the doors were locked, as if to deter would-be auto thieves.

She had driven around the building and was unsettled seeing there were no other vehicles, other than a public utility service van parked by an open sewer hole. Two men stood to either side of it. They were staring into the hole like they were waiting for something to emerge.

Mary was half expecting the front doors to be locked, but when she pulled on the handle of one, it swung open easily, and she stepped into the vestibule. Once she was inside the building proper, she saw a chubby woman at a front desk in a navy jacket and matching flowery bowtie.

"Thank you for choosing St. Eloise," the woman said. "What may I help you with today?" Her teeth were brilliantly white.

"I have an appointment with Dr. Rick...Dr. Rick...uhh..." Mary realized she didn't know her doctor's last name.

"Oh!" the woman chimed in. "If you'd just sign in here, you can go right up to the fourth floor."

"Oh. Okay." Mary stepped closer, picked up the pen attached to the clipboard in front of her, and signed. She looked up at the young woman, noticing her name tag. "You said the fourth floor, Maddy?"

"How'd you know my name?" Maddy asked with a start, the cheerful smile not falling from her face.

Mary nodded at the little plate pinned to her work jacket.

"Oh." Maddy giggled. "I forgot that was there. Just follow the sign."

Mary thought it was exactly the type of thing someone would do—trying to get a person to let their guard down before springing the trap. She smiled at the young woman and walked between two potted floor plants, en route to a bank of four elevators.

The appeal of the architecture of an older building was completely lost once she was inside. The paint on the walls was all sallow greens and yellows, with pictures of old men she'd never heard of and inscriptions of quotes they were supposed to be famous for saying. Mary pushed the up button, and one of the doors dinged when they slid open.

She stepped in the car decorated with faux wood panels and had to jam the button for the fourth floor four times before it lit. The doors ground closed, and after a second-and-a-half pause, the car jerked, lifting to her destination. Mary felt like she was being stretched through a pinhole for just a moment before the car slowed to a crawl, giving her a millisecond feel of freedom from the pull of gravity before the doors opened, settling the last few inches to her floor.

She cautiously stepped out of the elevator in front of a bland-looking white hall. A sign directly in front of her had Dr. Rick's name above an arrow pointing to the right. She went in that direction, following more signs leading her around in a maze-like pattern. Mary was reasonably certain the majority of the turns were redundant, that she was being led through an unnecessarily circuitous route, until she came to an office with his name in a glass window in the upper half of the door. She entered.

"Hi," a reddish-haired woman said from behind the counter.

Mary made a path toward the smiling woman and was about to reach for the sign-in sheet when the woman continued.

"I'll buzz you in. Just go to Exam Room Four."

The door buzzed to Mary's right. She walked over, twisted the knob, and pulled. It didn't open.

"Hold on," the woman said.

The door buzzed again and stopped. Mary pulled, but it didn't open.

"Wait a minute."

The door buzzed, but Mary was already pulling.

"Let go," the woman said. "I have to buzz first."

Mary nodded, pausing until the buzz. She yanked as soon as she heard it, but it stopped a millisecond before she pulled.

"Darn it," the woman said. "Hang on." Her head disappeared, and a moment later, she pushed the door open and let Mary inside. "It's the first room around the corner."

"Thank you," Mary said, then found her room.

She took off her jacket and laid her purse atop it in the chair. When she shut the door and turned to get on the examination table, a man was sitting in that chair, her purse and jacket in his lap.

"Oh my god!" Mary put a hand to her chest in surprise. "I didn't see you there."

He blinked, slowly turning his head in her direction as if he hadn't seen her before either. "Oh, Mrs. Walker," Dr. Rick said. He pushed his glasses up on his nose, noticing the items in his lap. Dr. Rick carefully picked up the items and stood, placing them back in the chair. "How are you today?"

She thought she was doing pretty well to not be in handcuffs right now, considering she had accidentally killed one of the nurses who worked here. "I'm fine." Mary forced herself to smile.

The swelling of her belly had continued, and she would have guessed she was at least four or five months pregnant. Dr. Rick put his hands on her shoulders, and Mary looked up to see him staring her in the eyes. She knew who he really was and felt a twinge of guilt, thinking of her ex.

"So, you killed my nurse. How's your appetite?" Dr. Rick asked.

"Good," she said. "A little morning sickness earlier today, but it went away. Do you want me to put on a gown or something?"

"Nah." Dr. Rick shook his head. "You're wearing a dress. That's good enough."

Mary would have worn pants, but the fact of it was, they didn't fit anymore. She hadn't worn this dress in at least a year and had forgotten it was even in her closet. It had been an impulse buy, and she'd immediately regretted it when she got home with it. Mary didn't like flowers. Why would she have purchased a flower-patterned dress?

Dr. Rick propped the upper half of the exam table to about thirty degrees. "Go ahead and have a seat and lay back." He washed his hands, dried them, and pulled on a pair of gloves.

Mary was waiting for him on the table, uncomfortable per her new usual. It no longer felt pleasant when she sat, as of a few hours ago.

The doctor took her pulse and listened to her heart and lungs, his face a mask of inexpression. He draped the stethoscope back over his neck and began feeling around on her belly.

"Little guy is starting to get active," Dr. Rick said.

"Guy?" Mary asked. "I'm having a boy?"

His eyebrows raised in surprise. "Oh, jeez, we never talked about that, did we? Do you *want* to have a boy?"

"I…I don't know." Mary hadn't given much thought to gender herself. She'd been so baby-obsessed, some of the details had gotten lost. Like the possibility of satan himself maybe being the father of her baby.

It definitely wasn't Walker's. She hadn't been intimate with him in almost a year.

Even though they'd separated on good terms and neither had any intention of being a couple again, for a little while, they'd continued having sex. That hadn't led to feelings being rekindled, but certain lines had been crossed. Like Walker wanting to spend the night. One day had been fine, but more than that and she knew he'd be angling to move in. She'd already bought the cow once and hadn't minded milking it on occasion, but seeing the cow's clothes all over the floor of her house had made her want to cut that cow into tender, juicy steaks, fillets, ribs, etc…

So that left the obvious. Derek. Well, there had been this *one* guy before she'd met Derek, but he'd been terrible in bed, so Mary decided he didn't count. Besides, that had been about ten months or so ago. Considering her gestation period just started yesterday, it had to be Derek's.

And he was so calm about the whole thing. Mary knew why she was pregnant, but it was still surprising how fast it was going. Yet, there was her rock. Derek never freaked out about anything. She'd never seen him upset, heard him raise his voice, or known of him being unkind to anybody.

And he didn't like porn. Mary had intentionally left out one of Walker's movies where Derek would find it—right next to the Keurig. He always got up at five in the morning—even now when he wasn't working—and had a couple of cups of coffee while he read the paper and then exercised. Mary didn't get up before nine unless she had specific reason to; the bank she worked for as a project manager had transitioned her to a home office when they'd moved to California, so they never started before eleven eastern time.

But the DVD had been gone. There was Derek, doing his exercises, the Keurig refilled and a new K-cup waiting for her to start it. Mary had rooted around in the trash later and found it in the bottom, the cover pulled out of the sleeve and balled up, the compact disc broken in two. He'd never brought it up.

So the baby had to be his. She and the devil—*Dr. Rick*, whatever his name was—had specifically agreed that he, the devil, would *not* be the father of her child. Mary was not up for a *Rosemary's Baby* situation, and he had assured her her child would be a hundred percent human. It still bugged her Dr. Rick hadn't told her who the baby's father was. If she could be so bold, why not ask now?"

"Doctor?" Mary began. "Is everything looking okay?"

He had moved up from examining her belly and was currently gently squeezing her left boob. It wasn't sexual in the least. From the look on his face, he wasn't taking any pleasure in it. But it also wasn't exactly clinical. She'd had many breast exams before, and no other doctor had done it quite like this.

"Hm, it seems so." He removed his hand. Dr. Rick paused for a long moment, putting a hand to his chin and twanging his soul patch with his index, looking a little lost. "As far as I can tell, you have a perfectly normal baby." He put his hands behind his back and rocked on his heels.

She was a little thrown off. This was her first pregnancy exam in a while, and there seemed to be...*stuff* he hadn't done. She couldn't say for sure what—Mary was pretty certain a pregnancy exam should take more than two minutes.

"Oh, would you like to know the baby's gender?"

"How could you know, though? I mean, isn't there a test you're supposed to do?"

"Right, right." Dr. Rick stared into the distance a moment. "I always forget that part." He grabbed a clipboard and then looked around the room. "Uh, you got a pen?"

"In my purse," Mary said, working up the nerve to ask her real question.

He seemed so disorganized. What kind of doctor didn't have something to write with?

The devil, that's who, she thought. It was easy to forget who he really was, or maybe he wielded some sort of magical charm, making people who knew forget. From the way he was acting, Mary wouldn't be surprised if some of that charm was at work on him too.

Dr. Rick rooted through her purse, somehow reaching his arm in up to the shoulder. He eventually pulled out a pen Mary was sure she hadn't seen in almost twenty years. It was a fancy blue and gold pen used for calligraphy her father had bought her as a high school graduation present. She'd lost it before she'd started college and had purchased the purse two years ago.

"So...would you like to know?" Dr. Rick asked again.

Mary desperately wanted to ask him to tell her everything he knew about the baby, but she and Derek had discussed and agreed it would be best for them to be surprised. They—well, Mary and subsequently Derek—wanted the mystery to be part of the story they eventually told the baby.

"I don't want to know the gender," Mary said. "But..."

He looked up from what he was writing. "But what?"

She forced the question out before she could think about it anymore. "Can you tell me who the father is?"

"The father?" Dr. Rick set the clipboard and pen aside, smiling like he was keeping a secret. "I'll do you one better. I'll let you *speak* to him." He reached past the clipboard and picked up a brown push button phone off the little counter.

Mary was certain it hadn't been there a second before. Dr. Rick sat in his rollaway chair and picked up the handset, grasping it with three fingers and using his index to push buttons.

"Oh, crap. I forgot to dial nine." He pressed one of the buttons on the cradle and started again, his mouth moving while he pressed each button. "Hey, Maddy, I need you to put somebody on the phone. I don't want to say his name—it's a surprise…No, not for you…No. He's in the room with that old guy…No, not him…Not him…Not him…Yeah, no-no…Not him, the other one…Thomas T. Telford…No, not Telford. The guy in the room with him…Well, I said it was a surprise. Can you just put him on?…What? No, I wasn't…I was *not*."

Dr. Rick took a deep breath before he continued, looking at Mary and rolling his eyes.

"Okay. I am sorry." A short pause. "For raising my tone. Yes. Yes, yes. Oh, he's with Dr. Saranc? That's actually perfect. *Thank you!*"

Dr. Rick looked at Mary and smiled.

"Just a moment. She's transferring me."

Mary had a growing sense of dread. Even though she had asked the question, it had since changed shape in her mind, and she was more interested in knowing who her baby's father *wasn't*. But she had bitten off this chunk and was going to have to swallow it.

"Hi, this is Dr. Rick. Dr. Saranc, please…Okay, okay. I know she's in with a patient. I need you to go in there and tell her to pick up the phone when you transfer me back…Yes, you are…Yes, you will. Because it's *me* you're talking to." He began nodding slowly. "Yessssss. *That* me."

a lowercase hell

Dr. Rick had his back to Mary, but she imagined his forked tongue flicking out of his mouth. He spun around and held up an index to Mary, followed by thirty-two seconds of silence.

"Dr. Saranc! Dr. Rick here...I know you're with a patient...I know. I know. It couldn't wait, though. Put him on the phone...No, it *can't* wait. I'm with a patient...Yes, I *can* appreciate the irony, but I don't appreciate your tone."

Dr. Rick stood, his skin suddenly crimson. A wreath of S-shaped horns curled up from his head. The lights went out, save for a bit illuminating him from beneath.

"Put him on the fucking phone now, or I will devour that boy of yours from the inside out with baby utensils!"

And then he was back to his Dr. Rick self.

He cleared his throat. "Thank you." After a short pause. "Hey, buddy. How ya doin'? Just gettin' a little therapy, huh? Well, look. I have someone who wants to talk to you here. Oh, it's somebody you know. H-hang on, m'kay?

Dr. Rick handed the handset over to Mary, doing his best to untangle the coiled spiral cord.

"Huh-hello?" Mary said.

"...Mary?" The line was staticky, but her heart still sank when she recognized Walker's voice. "Mary, where are you? Are you okay? Are you alive?"

Tears filtered her vision. She tried to speak, but she couldn't tell if she was actually making sounds, let alone words. Mary had loved this man once, and some aspect of her always would. Didn't

59

his eternal soul have more worth than just to be traded for a baby? How could she blame him for something that had been lacking in *her* body?

"I'm-I'm sorry. Walker, I'm sorry," she heard herself say, her throat in a knot. "So sorry. So-so Sorry."

"Mary—" A wave of static wiped out his voice. "Mary, are you there?"

"It's all my fault." Her voice was coming out clearly, but it wasn't her talking. Mary sobbed, her body shaking. She drew in breaths of razor blades and breathed out around a lava-hot stone caught in her throat. "I'm the one who sent you to hell," she said in the voice that was and wasn't hers. "I traded you for the baby I always wanted. It was the least you could do, after all the pain you caused me."

"No!" Mary shouted, pulling the phone away from her face. "I didn't say that. I didn't mean—"

The phone line crowded with static again and went dead.

Dr. Rick had the biggest smile she'd ever seen on a human face.

Chapter 9. Second Heaven

So this was the city. Alfred surveyed the
streets of gold and the buildings—some made of
ivory, some built right into the trunks of the massive
trees in abundance here. He shook his head,
thinking even heaven was cliché. What would this
place be to someone who had fought the ivory trade
all his life? Or a Forty-Niner who had spent his last
years and scraps of fortune to only find a few flakes
of gold before he starved to death, alone in the
middle of nowhere? Would this not be a hell for
them?

He had pieced Hammercock back together,
and the man had gone on whining long after his
body had knitted together again. Alfred had no
intention of wasting any of his meager resources. If
he was going to make an affront to heaven, he
couldn't afford to squander anything. Even a pissant
like the broken-down-actor-turned-detective.

At least this section of the city reminded him
of the Piazza della Signoria, except the buildings
were ivory instead of red and brown brick. He
strolled onto a path, feeling a warm sense of at-
homeness. Alfred had never experienced such a
thing before, the sensation vibrating up his legs and
into his groin, like he was being wrapped in a hug
from the feet up.

It was all he could do to keep from
screaming and running back the way he'd come. In
life, no place had ever been home for Alfred. He'd
known from an early age he hadn't belonged
anywhere. Until he'd actually died and been cast up

to heaven, he'd never known anything as near to god-like as him. Just because he now had been confronted by winged beings of untold strength did not give him a moment's doubt of his opinion of himself. They were just another species he'd yet to conquer.

There was an old man standing behind a cart with three melon-like globes atop it. The old man was nearly bald, his scalp half covered in liver spots, with a grayish-white beard nearly half the length of his white-white tunic. Curious, Alfred approached.

"What do you have, old man?"

"It's a special melon I grew just this morning!"

The sparse few teeth Alfred had been able to make out were yellow and worn. Alfred wondered how the man could have such an appearance in heaven. He should have been beautiful and perfect, life's maladies left behind with life. Alfred decided to ponder that later.

"This…morning?" he asked, also wondering why anyone would bother working in heaven.

The old man nodded, his smile widening to show even more gaps in his mouth.

"How much?"

The old man's face fell, his eyebrows coming together as if he didn't understand the question. Alfred poked one melon with his index and spoke.

"How much do these melons cost?"

"I don't…" The old man looked around like he was searching for someone to explain.

"Atta, this one is asking you to barter with him."

Alfred turned, seeing the biggest angel yet since he'd come to heaven. This one could probably smash the first two's heads together. The angel looked at Alfred.

"Take a look around, small one. All the riches one could desire are here in abundance. There is no value in buying or selling. The work is its own reward."

"So…they're free?" Alfred asked, barely stifling a laugh. "You did this—what—out of the kindness of your heart?"

"No. The labor is my recompense," Atta, the old man, said.

The word *recompense* made Alfred wonder what language they were both speaking. To his ears, the old man had used perfectly unaccented American English. The angel sounded British. Come to think of it, the other two angels had sounded British too. He wondered what language they heard when he spoke.

"So, I may have this?" Alfred picked up the center melon, a light-yellow globe a little smaller than a bowling ball. He raised it to his mouth.

"Not the whole…thing," Atta said when Alfred took a bite.

Alfred locked eyes with the old man, slowly chewing. The flood of sweetness drenching his mouth was almost overwhelming. It was the most delicious thing Alfred had ever eaten. Tears sprang to his eye, and it was all he could do not to choke on the juice washing down his throat.

Atta's smile had returned, and the angel was looking at Alfred too. "How was it?" the angel asked.

"It's like a party in my mouth," Alfred replied, a small amount of the juice flowing down the wrong pipe and giving him a coughing fit. "And everybody's dancing!"

The old man nodded, proud of his work.

"Jason Stillmore sucked on my pee-pee when we was twelve!" the melon in Alfred's hand shouted.

Alfred's eyes went wide, and he looked at it. "Did that—" he began.

"I told him I'd do him after, but I was lyin'!"

Atta seemed unperturbed by this, but Alfred was horrified.

"What the hell is this?" Alfred shook the melon as if that would shut it up.

"It's a Yellin' Melon," the old man said. "If it tastes sweet, it shouts something you are proud of."

"Proud?" Alfred was flabbergasted. "Why would—"

"I made somethin' called booger sauce. Err'body ate it!"

Okay, Alfred had been proud of that one. But he didn't like the melon sharing his secrets.

"Ma'am Davis let me pull on her titties!"

Okay, that *was enough.*

Alfred dropped the melon on the golden street and, before anyone could say anything— *especially the melon*—crushed it underfoot.

64

"Oh no." Atta's curled back bowed even further. Then he reached into a shelf on the cart and drew out another melon.

"Fret not, Atta," the angel said. "I shall have one as well. And I will not waste a drop."

"Thank you, Gamael."

The giant angel picked up the new melon with his thumb and middle finger. He brought it to his meaty lips and took a bite, giving Alfred the impression he could have stuffed the whole thing in with room to spare.

"I like to edge, then squeeze my knob 'til it goes numb!" the melon shouted.

"De*li*cious," Gamael said.

Hammercock limped over. He reached and Alfred slapped his hand.

"Not for you!" Alfred had no idea why the man limped. The angels had torn off his arms, not his legs. "You'll eat when I say."

"Yes, angel."

"I have plenty. He may have some." Atta held his hands out pleadingly.

"No, he's got a gluten sensitivity," Alfred said. "Say, would either of you be able to tell me where the nearest library is?"

"I broke a table with my schwantz on a dare!" the melon said when Gamael slid the rest of it in his mouth.

It mumbled something more, but Alfred couldn't make it out.

"I can take you there, if it pleases you," the giant angel said. "The battle is not for a time yet."

"Then we'll follow you," Alfred replied.

"Follow?" Gamael asked. "I said I'd take you."

Before Alfred could respond, Gamael stepped forward and grabbed him and Hammercock. His mighty wings sprouted from his back and, with one mighty flap, heaved all three of them into the sky.

Chapter 10. Not All Demons Look Alike

"So where are you from?" Median asked "Fred," the nurse wheeling him to his appointment. He was still pretty fascinated by the idea of cities in hell.

"Stygia Township," the nurse said.

Median looked over his shoulder when the demon let go of the handles of the wheelchair long enough to dislocate the joints of three of his four fingers into an "S". "S-siiiiide!"

"Is everybody green where you're from?"

The nurse narrowed his eyes at Median. "What are you, some kind of racist? My mom's red, man."

"I'm sorry."

"Sorry? The fuck do you mean by that? You saying you're sorry because my mom's red or because I'm green?"

Median felt like he was caught in a trap.

"I'm sorry if I offended you." He faced forward. "I really don't know racial dynamics down here. Green, red, purple—none is better than another as far as I'm concerned. Although, if there is one group that is systematically targeted and oppressed, then everyone should acknowledge that and make strides to level the playing field."

"That's right," the nurse said after a long moment. "Now the fuck do you mean by 'down here'?"

"I'll take him from here," a woman said just ahead of them in the hall. She had on an ash-gray jacket and matching pencil skirt, her auburn hair pinned up and a pair of square-framed glasses on her sharp face.

"Yes, ma'am." Fred let go of the wheelchair's handles.

The woman resumed his place, pushing Median toward a large wooden office door in the middle of the hall T-boning the one they were in. To either side, there were no other doors, and the adjacent hall stretched at least fifty feet in either direction.

Median thought she might stop to open the door or maybe he might offer to get up and open it. Hell, it was his arm that had been injured, not his legs. But she kept walking until his feet were about a yard away, and the door swung inward. She wheeled him inside, and the door shut.

Everything in here was brown. It was an expansive room, but Median still would have guessed the hallway was wider. It had to have been some sort of addition—he'd been on other floors, and the ceilings were all relatively low, but this room's ceiling was easily twenty feet high or more.

He'd never seen wall paneling like this outside of a movie. It was all inlaid squares, about three inches by three inches, with bookshelves on every wall stretching to the ceiling, except for the window directly ahead of him, taking up the whole wall.

The woman turned him toward a large burnt-oak desk which only had a picture of a handsome young white kid in a football jersey. Median thought the boy's face was more of a squared version of hers once she came around the desk. She smoothed down the front of her skirt and sat.

"I'm Dr. Sinclair Saranc." She picked up a glass of ice water he hadn't seen a second before and sipped. Dr. Saranc placed it gingerly on a coaster, which he was certain had appeared just as she sat the glass down. "I'm sorry, would you like anything before we begin? Water or tea or Red Rocket Pop?"

"Oh, no, thanks." Median waved her off. "I've had enough for today."

"All right," Dr. Saranc said, nodding. "I've read your file, Mr. Harris, but is there anything you would like for me to know in particular before we begin?"

"My file?" Median was confused. "Is this a therapy session? I thought I was here for my arm." He held up his bandaged limb and pointed to it with his other hand.

"This is a regular part of intake for anyone who comes through here."

"You know, my roommate said it's not common to come straight here. That usually people—*souls*—go to hell first and *then* come here."

Dr. Saranc raised her trimmed eyebrows. "Well, your roommate is *a patient* here. I'm actually a staff member. It is true that most patients come here after going to hell proper, but patients in your situation aren't all that uncommon."

"My…*situation*?" The word scared Median as much as it gave him a meandering sense of hope.

"I apologize, but I'm a little loath to say. It would be best for you to reach the conclusion on your own."

"Okay," Median replied after a long moment. He'd been to therapy before. Once when he was in his teens, much to his mother's disagreement—*What do you need a psychiatrist for? Just for her to fill your mind up with how much I screwed you up? I'm a good mother, and you have nothing to complain about!*—and on two separate occasions while he and Mary had been together.

"Let's just say there are certain things you haven't dealt with in your former life that perhaps we could start now."

"But I'm *dead* now."

"And what makes you say that?" Dr. Saranc steepled her fingers and put her indexes to her nose. The gesture looked very contemplative.

"Because...I'm in hell?"

She shrugged and made some noncommittal facial expression. "Let's just say better late than never."

A corner of Dr. Saranc's mouth lifted in a smile. Median didn't respond, not knowing how.

"I apologize. My little version of a joke. Any place you'd like to dive into first?"

"No." Median shook his head. "Not really."

"Okay. Why don't we start with what you do for a living? *Did.*"

Median thought. He'd had a lot of odd jobs in his life. "Most recently, I was doing some customer service work for this mortgage company. Mostly second shift."

"Okay. Why don't we start with how you got into the adult film industry?"

"Oh. That." The way she cut to the chase made him think this was the only thing she wanted to talk about. Median's cheeks burned, and he shrugged his shoulders so hard he felt like he was twelve for a moment. "You know about that? Not a...not a lot of people do."

"Let's just say we start there. Why do you want people not to know you perform in pornographic films?"

Perform in pornographic films. Median made a face.

"What?" Dr. Saranc asked.

"*What* what?" Median asked.

"You made a face, Mr. Harris. Let's just say it was telling me something. Could you put that message into words?"

"*Let's just say*—" Median shook his head. "Nobody says it that way. 'Perform in pornographic films.' I have sex on camera, or I do fuck-films. I cum for the credits. Okay, I made that last one up, but 'perform in pornographic films' sounds like how someone whose native language is French would say it."

Dr. Saranc wrote something down in the notepad that was suddenly in her hands.

Median adjusted in his chair. "I suppose I got started...more or less on a dare." Median let his thoughts roam, remembering a jumble of events leading up to his first appearance on camera. "Yeah. I guess a dare would be the best way to phrase it."

"Was your...I suppose you'd call it, your side career, the reason for the breakdown of your marriage?"

"No," Median said quickly, shaking his head. "No. We were already done by then."

"I see." The doctor wrote something else. "So tell me the story. I'm sure you can understand what someone on my side of it might think. A married man getting into performing—being an adult film star..." She held her hands out.

"Well, I wouldn't call myself a *star*," Median replied.

She cocked an eyebrow at him. He'd already noticed the doctor was an attractive woman, showing off a lot of cleavage with her button-up shirt and tight skirt, but it was more the subtle things that initiated his attraction to a woman. The way she was looking at him now made it necessary for Median to cross his legs so as not to "tip his hand" so to speak, wearing nothing but the open-backed gown he'd had on since he got here.

He cleared his throat and continued. "Okay. So I said it was kind of a dare, and that's true, but that isn't how they found me. I...made a video for my wife on my phone when she was away on business. Y'know, to let her know how much I was missing her. I've always been sort of an exhibitionist, and as soon as the idea hit me, I didn't think twice about it. I sent it to her, but I guess after it got uploaded to the cloud..."

"Somebody found it. Did she enjoy the video?"

"Uh, yeah." Median was surprised by the question. So much had happened because the video had gotten out of his control, he sort of looked at its originally intended purpose as secondary. "She showed me how much after she came back home a couple nights later."

Median took a moment to reminisce over the long-neglected memory before his eyes flicked up to Dr. Saranc, who was nodding patiently at him and tapping the end of her pen against her supple lower lip.

"So, I don't know. Maybe a month or two later, a friend of mine called me and told me about this video he saw on a porn site. He asked if it was me, and I told him I didn't know what he was talking about. He gave me the site, and I went on…I was mortified. I mean, my parents, y'know?"

"And why were they a concern? Do your parents watch adult films?"

That hit Median like a slap in the face. He wanted to say no, but he didn't honestly know. Thinking about it now and what he knew about them…he'd have to guess they probably did. His mind drifted to that last phone call. What had they been up to?

"I don't think so." Median didn't consider it a lie when he had no real way of knowing.

"But by the look on your face, you wouldn't be exactly surprised?"

Median opened his mouth to answer and realized he didn't know what to say. He'd seen…things his parents did when he was a child which now flashed to his mind, leading him to believe they might have been into more than he wanted to acknowledge.

"Shit, this is hell, right? Why am I being shy?" Median said. "I found...not a dildo, but some sort of studded thing in my parents' closet when I was ten while they were away. I had no clue what it was, except that I was sure I wasn't supposed to see it. I mean, I've never used whatever that thing was on anybody, even in porn, but I guess it was something that he put on himself and used on her."

His mind reeled from saying the words out loud.

"But you knew it was sexual in nature?"

"Yeah, I guess."

"Were there other incidents or...discoveries?"

Median thought a moment. "I mean, yeah, but what kid hasn't seen their parents do—y'know—stuff?"

"Fair point, but how often would you say you saw your parents making sweet, sweet love, and was it ever at your expense?"

"My expense?" Median almost didn't understand the question. But then he recalled how his parents had had a *lot* of sex when he was growing up. They had always supported him by coming to little league games or taking him to comic book conventions, but he'd become so accustomed to their overt sexuality that when they'd disappeared from the stands or had to use the restroom at the exact same time and were gone for ten minutes or more, he'd known they were more than likely doing it. "I guess at times."

"Give me a number," Dr. Saranc said. "Your best guess."

"Since I've been aware?" Median did a gross tally in his head. And he couldn't help but include the last conversation in which his mother had rushed him off the phone. "Maybe six hundred-ish?"

"I…" The doctor's mouth fell open.

"Is that a lot?"

She quickly recovered, narrowing her eyes. "The fact you'd ask that question is sort of telling, don't you think?" Dr. Saranc picked up her notepad and began furiously scribbling.

"If you say so."

"Did your parents get into swinging, threesomes, pegging, or any other communal sexual activities?"

He shook his head. "How would I know that?" But he did recall a woman hanging around the house when he was eight or so.

She'd come over at night and sometimes still be there in the morning. There was a guy later on too. Auntie Janet and Uncle Jacob, his parents had said to call them. But they weren't married. And as far as he knew, Jacob wasn't his uncle at all. He had been Jewish, and both sides of Median's family were Baptist.

Median stayed silent instead of mentioning any of this.

"What effect do you think your parents' activities might have had on yours as an adult?"

He laughed. "Oh man, you really think that? Life doesn't happen in straight lines, Dr…Dr…"

"Saranc."

"Dr. Saranc. Could it have had an impact? Sure. Is it the only reason? Of course not. Look, I was always taking off my clothes when I was a kid. My grandpa always said I had a great body."

"Your grandfather?"

"Don't get any ideas. He was a sculptor. He saw the beauty in just about everything. He thought my mom had a great body too. I think my parents still have the statue he made of her when she was a teenager.

"At any rate, it was tough for my parents to keep my clothes on until I was about six or seven. I probably exposed myself to my whole classroom in kindergarten at least three times."

"Walker, why do you think your marriage failed?"

Median rolled his eyes at the sudden turn in conversation. "I don't want to talk about that."

"You don't think it had anything to do with your erstwhile vocation?"

"No, I told you I didn't get involved in that until after we'd split up."

"But what about before you split up? What happened?"

Median's temper begin to boil, but then, just like that, he was fine. He was in hell. Probably was going to be here for a long time. Why *not* tell her?

"To oversimplify it, my wife cheated on me. But it wasn't her fault."

"Please," Dr. Saranc said, "go on."

"I don't know what it was. For the first couple years, our intimacy was okay. I mean, once or twice a week."

"And you were how old when you got married?"

"I was twenty-one. She was twenty."

"Once or twice a week in your early twenties? I'd say that's probably below average."

"Okay. Yeah. She pretty much said that too." Median waved his hands in the air in frustration. "And gradually, twice a week turned into once, and then once turned to none."

"You just lost interest in her?"

"That's the thing." Median shook his head. "Mary is probably the sexiest woman I've ever been with. And I've been with some pretty hot women in porn. And all the time, while we were still together, I still took care of business myself, y'know?"

Dr. Saranc nodded as if she had had a thought.

"What?"

"Have you ever heard of allodynia?"

Median shook his head. "Uh-uh."

"It's an aversion to sexual intimacy. Not necessarily fear of the sexual act itself, but the emotion attached to it in combination."

"Oh." He thought about that for a moment. "What causes that?"

"Like you said, there's not a straight line from one thing to another. Outside of your wife, how many long-term relationships have you had?"

"None. In high school, I hooked up with a few girls, but that was about it. I'd say before porn I'd been with about four women?"

"Any men?"

Median was about to answer when the phone rang.

"Walker, I apologize. My assistant knows to hold my calls."

She picked up.

"Hello? I'm with a patient. I can't take interruptions in the middle of a session…Do what?…Absolutely not. Whatever you have to say can wait…Oh, you are, are you? Can you appreciate the irony?…I'm not interested in playing whatever game this is—"

The voice on the other end got loud enough for Median to hear it but not understand.

"I can do that. I understand. But I'd like my complaint noted."

She held the phone out to Median.

"It's for you."

He made a face but leaned forward to take the handset from her. Median recognized the ridiculousness when he half rose from his wheelchair to grab it.

"Hello?" he said.

"Hey, buddy. How ya doin'?" came the staticky voice on the other end.

"Dr. Rick?"

"Just gettin' a little therapy, huh? Well, look. I have someone who wants to talk to you here."

"To me? Who?"

"Oh, it's somebody you know. H-hang on, m'kay?"

Median listened to the phone being fumbled.

"Huh-hello?" someone said through the static.

"...Mary?" He couldn't believe it was her. This had to be some sort of torture, but he didn't care. Her voice was like rain in the desert. "Mary, where are you? Are you okay? Are you alive?"

Median's eyes began watering. He thumbed his nose, feeling like it had started running. He hadn't believed in hell or the devil a few days ago. But now he'd been presented irrefutable proof, it was all he could hope for that the people he cared about weren't down here with him.

"I'm-I'm sorry. Walker, I'm sorry." Mary sounded like she was crying. "So sorry. So-so sorry."

He had no idea what she was apologizing for. If it hadn't been for Mary, he and Joe would have died in that building. They'd all barely survived, even with her help. It wasn't her fault he'd died on the operating table. She'd gotten him to the hospital. Median's mind went to his parents. They needed to know he was dead, and he needed to know they were all right.

"Mary, could you check on my folks?" There was a storm of static when he spoke, making him pull the phone away from his ear for a moment. "Mary, are you there?"

"It's all my fault," she said, her voice flat. She'd sounded like she'd been crying a moment before, but now she was calm. "I'm the one who

79

sent you to hell. I traded you for the baby I always wanted. It was the least you could do, after all the pain you caused me."

"Mary, what are you saying? I died on the operating table, didn't I?"

"No!" Mary shouted. Then her voice was farther away, like someone had taken the phone away from her. "I didn't say that. I didn't mean—"

Static rose again, and the line went dead.

"Hello?" Median had a sinking sensation in his gut. "Hello?"

Dr. Saranc gently took the handset away and placed it back in the cradle. Median blinked at her. She hadn't gotten up from her chair, and her arms didn't look long enough to reach him.

"What the hell was that?" he asked.

"It's exactly what it sounded like." Dr. Saranc stared at him as if waiting for Median to catch up. "Let me clear up one thing for you, Walker. You aren't dead."

"What do you mean, I'm not dead? Of course, I am. I'm in hell."

"Job walked into heaven without ever dying. What makes you think the same can't happen here?"

Median was about to answer, but as blank spaces filled in within his mind, he realized a few things.

Mary had betrayed him. Twice.

If she were pregnant, that was what she'd gotten out of it. But what did the devil get for taking him alive?

a lowercase hell

"Why am I here?" he asked Dr. Saranc, his
voice fragile. "I mean, alive. Why was I brought
here without dying? It would have been easy for me
to die—I had a big-ass knife in my arm. Why bother
doing the surgery to save me if I was just coming to
hell anyway?"

Dr. Saranc nodded thoughtfully, waiting for
him to finish. "This isn't exactly how I wanted to
tell you this, but you were going to find out soon
enough. Your wife exchanged you for the life
growing inside her right now. In exchange, the devil
gets to eat you. On his wedding day."

Chapter 11. Detroit Monster Mamas

Mary had gone from being terrified of the devil telling her he knew she had killed Mrs. Manhorn to the horror of her worst secret being revealed to the one person she had feared learning it the most.

She'd betrayed the man she had once loved. Still loved, but just…not like that.

Mary had called Derek as soon as she'd gotten back to her car, crying. He'd listened patiently until she'd been able to get the words out. She found his complete silence throughout the whole ordeal comforting.

"I need you," she'd told him.

"Okay," he'd said before she'd even indicated what for.

Dr. Rick, despite his odd methods—and the fact he was the malebolgia—had returned to normal once he'd hung up the phone. He prescribed her some prenatal vitamins, thought better of it, then gave her a couple of samples he had up front. After all, she was going to have this baby tomorrow.

He'd suggested a Lamaze class to help her with breathing and controlling pain. When Mary'd mentioned to Derek there was a class in a little over a half hour, he'd dropped everything to meet her there.

She had never heard of the place, but it was easy enough to find. It was just off the Lodge Freeway, on the west side, and by the time she got there, her bulky fiancé, staring into space, was leaning against his truck.

"Baby!" he said when he saw her.

Mary practically leapt into his arms, and yet again, the strength emanating from this man made most of her fears melt away.

"I love you, Derek," she said, holding him so tight he was the one who grunted in pain.

His ribs were still healing. Despite his look of nigh-indestructibility, he wasn't.

They walked hand in hand into the squat, single-story building. The interior was a mix of pinks and blues, with cartoonish drawings of babies and Roman-esque mothers either holding them or allowing them to breastfeed while they stared, white-eyed, at nothing.

"I need to call my mom," Derek said.

A woman at the front desk gave them directions to the classroom, and they quickly found it, with about a half dozen other expectant mothers. The women were all seated in a semicircle on a thick-carpeted floor. A few were conversing. The pregnant woman near where they sat looked at them with big violet eyes.

"Oh my, Dad's here?" she said and giggled.

Mary and Derek scooched around until they were in-line with the rest of the semicircle.

"Hi. I'm Mary. This is my fiancé, Derek."

"I'm Cassandra," the woman said, and she and Mary shook hands.

When Derek held out his hand, Cassandra pulled him into a hug. He stiffened, then relaxed, and she took a deep breath of him. Mary didn't like it, but she wasn't exactly about to start a fight with the woman.

"Nice to meet you, Sandy," Derek said.

Mary elbowed him in the ribs, and he hissed an intake of air.

"When are you due?" Cassandra asked. She looked ready to pop any moment.

"Tomorrow." Mary felt a sense of superiority for some strange reason.

"Oh, really? You don't look six months, even."

"I'm only two days." Mary didn't know why she was being petty. It definitely wasn't like her.

Derek put a hand over hers as if to calm her. She barely resisted the urge to rake her fingernails down his face.

"Good afternoon, ladies!" someone said from the back of the room. A tall, dark-skinned woman with close-cropped, salt and pepper curls walked around the semicircle, wearing striped black and white leggings and an oversized orange, sleeveless top. "Welcome, welcome. New faces and familiar, I'm Fariah. Like Mariah but with an 'F'."

She was gorgeous—high cheekbones, full lips, hazel eyes that seemed to glow against her skin. Mary couldn't guess her age, but there was an energy about her that told Mary she was easily the wisest woman in the room.

"And gentleman," the woman said, effortlessly dropping into a cross-legged seated position. She smiled at Derek and cocked her head to the side. "Are you sure you want to be in here?"

"Uh, yeah?" Derek replied.

"Are you *sure*?"

Mary couldn't quite figure the expression on Derek's face. Not that he'd had a tremendous range of emotion, but her best guess was this was a look of embarrassment. And she couldn't figure for the life of her why he would have such a look on his face, like one of the women in here had a boob hanging out.

He looked around and licked his lips.

"Honey, are you okay?" Mary asked. "If you need to wait out in the lobby, that's—"

"Okay." Derek shot up, one of Mary's hands still in his. He bent and kissed it as an afterthought and quickly fled the room.

"Now that the old ball and chain is gone, let's get started!" Fariah said once the door had shut behind Derek.

The other women laughed and began scooching in closer to the instructor. Mary hesitantly followed suit.

"Nothing personal, but I find men don't do so well in this class. Especially…y'know…" She shook her head and smiled.

"No, I don't know. What do you mean?" Mary asked.

"That he isn't the father. I mean, half the ladies here have someone, and they've all been josephed."

"Josephed? I don't understand."

"Your baby. It's not his. Some god or devil impregnated you too, right?"

"What? Why would you think that?" Mary drew back in revulsion.

"It's not a big deal. All the ladies here are in your situation."

"I am the fifty-first wife of Lord Vlatep," said a smiling dark-skinned woman with silver hair and silvery-blue eyes. "The four of us were on our honeymoon, when he was killed right in front of me by the second troika—his second set of wives. Two of them held him down while the third pulled his spine out through his stomach. They slaughtered his other two brides too. I barely survived." She giggled. "Luckily, I was able to consummate with him." She put a hand on her belly and thrust her chin out. "I shall give birth to the next queen."

"I was josephed," a waif of a woman said, raising her hand. "I don't know which creature got me pregnant. I tried to have an abortion, but it…ate the doctor."

A few of the women gasped.

"I…I think it's going to eat me too."

"Look, I don't know what situation you mean," Mary said. "I am *not* pregnant with the devil's baby. I haven't been josephed. I've been dereked. Derek is the father of my baby." Mary struggled to stand. When she finally got up, she was panting—her belly must have gotten bigger since she walked in this place—and felt prickles of sweat on her brow and lower back. "I think there's been some sort of mistake. I don't think I belong here."

"I'm sorry. I'm sorry." Fariah stood, holding her hands out in surrender. "There are no judgments here. The only thing I want to do is help you when it comes to delivering your baby."

Mary was already retreating toward the door. It wasn't Fariah or the other women—well, it wasn't *only* them. The doctor appointment and the phone call were a big factor in her freaking out right now. She only wanted to get home, curl up with Derek, and watch Netflix.

"No-no, it's not you," Mary began. She didn't know how to finish her statement, though. "It's just, I can't...I can't...I'm sorry. Thank you." She left the room and walked as quickly as she could without running toward the front door.

The lights flickered and went out. A milky brightness outlined a door at the beginning of a hall. It was not only brilliant but seemed to be pulsing. Mary found herself unable to resist this light and had to know what it was coming from.

She put her hand on the doorknob, feeling *something* powerful enough to vibrate through the floor on the other side. The tiny hairs on her forearms stood on end. She felt a moment's fear before turning the knob and pushing inside.

Mary was shocked and horrified to see the young woman, who'd been behind the greeting desk, on her knees before a glowing, shirtless Derek. He had his head thrown back as if in delight, and the young woman was prostrate, her head touching the floor, her outstretched hands touching his bare feet.

"What the hell is this?" Mary shouted.

Immediately, Derek stopped glowing and whirled around.

"Mary!" he said, excited, although his pupils were dilated. "It's not what it looks like. I swear, I can explain."

"Was she…" Mary began, realizing what she'd seen. "Was she *worshipping* you?"

Chapter 12. Library

Alfred hadn't been able to find anything of value in the library. After talking Gamael down from believing he was going to "take" both he and Hammercock, the angel had flown off in a huff, his might wings almost knocking the two men over from the gust before they went inside. The angel had done nothing to contain his mystery—his skirts had opened several times, revealing a flaccid penis that could have easily doubled as a tree stump.

It was all bibles as soon as they'd walked in the vestibule, with modest little shelves doubling as one-person benches. The design of the interior was just as impressive as the outside, and by his keen eye, Alfred detected everything had been carved by hand. But Alfred hadn't come here for the architecture. He saw right away that coming here had been a mistake.

Once they were in the library proper, there were more shelves with more bibles, all different versions—King James, Bishop's Bible, Living English, Christian Community Bible, Aldhelm, Psalters, Farman, Ælfric…King Alfred—that caught his eye for a moment, but he was quickly bored,

He was fluent in more than thirty languages and could at least recognize many more, but there were symbols he'd never seen on the spines of some of these, and he was pretty certain some weren't human languages at all.

"All the answers a body could yearn for, right, Angel?" Hammercock asked him.

"Shut up," Alfred had said. He would have struck the old man dead at that point had he been able. Sycophants only appealed to him for so long, and the validation ego-stroking provided had long lost its value. He didn't want to just turn him loose, though. Dissolution of faith was how gods perished, usually by the bloodied hands of their congregation. He would swallow his revulsion of Hammercock until he could make permanent use of him.

They sat outside on the steps of the library. Alfred couldn't even ask an angel for guidance, limited as it probably would have been. The few dozen they'd seen all had been in a rush to be elsewhere. There was supposed to be some pending battle or other. In hindsight, Alfred should have known the secrets to heaven wouldn't be kept in a library. He had to think of something but wasn't sure where to begin.

The angels were no good. They thought of humans as playthings—or worse, sex objects. There were people milling about, but what could they know more than him? Other than his strange melons, Atta had been an idiot, and Alfred was certain no other person would fare better. He was also sure that if god were here at all, he would be the absolute worst one to speak with. If he was as all-powerful and all-knowing as he was alleged to be in his biography, then Alfred's scheme would be dashed in the snap of a finger.

But then again…if god was as all-powerful and all-knowing as he was alleged to be, wouldn't he have already known what Alfred was up to? When he turned it over and over in his mind, there were only three options: god was real and he didn't care, was just as interested to see what would happen next, or he wasn't real and Alfred could do what he wanted.

Alfred looked across the narrow cobblestone path. A man had raised his tunic, holding the bottom to his chest while he cradled his arm around a tree. His hips mechanically worked back and forth, thrusting into it. Alfred looked at the man making love to the tree curiously, amazed he wasn't offended in the least.

"Wait," Alfred said, putting a hand on Hammercock's leg. "This is heaven."

"*Yes*," Hammercock said, his voice husky.

Alfred turned to him. The old man had a look of lust in his eyes because of where Alfred's hand was midway up on his thigh. Even Alfred's revulsion at this man was lessened. He'd been pansexual in life, and his lack of attraction to the old man had more to do with Hammercock's self-delusion. Alfred had used that attraction to his advantage and then had been glad to be rid of him. Had they not been where they were now, he would have killed Hammercock, but Alfred didn't *want* to.

"Heaven is only heaven if you can do what you want," Alfred said. "Have what you want. All desire fulfilled." The man with the tree began moaning loudly between sloppy kisses he placed on the bark, and Alfred was surprised the tree cried out in ecstasy. "Everything here bends to the will of man. And everyone here is a buffoon. I need...I need to go to the head of them all. I need the King of the Idiots. Those angels before...they said they were going to see the 'first one'. What was his name again?"

Alfred already knew, but he felt he was on a roll.

"I-I don't remember," Hammercock said. The old man's eyes rolled back into his head, and he began gyrating, pitching a tent in his tunic.

No, that didn't bother Alfred either, even though in life he had been repulsed by other people's orgasms. The man with the tree had finished also and was lying on the grass in front of it with a piece of fruit that had fallen from a branch.

"I need Morgan."

Chapter 13. Vote for Doolot

Median had been relatively sure the nurse who came to take him back to his room had been Fred, but the name tag on his jacket read "George". After the minor debacle of their last meeting, he didn't want to get looped into another bout of the "Do you think we all look alike?" encounter.

George helped him go to the restroom, even though Median's legs worked perfectly fine. Median smiled at him once he'd flushed, making sure to use the grab bars to stand and move to the sink to wash his hands. Then George scooped him up in his arms and carried him to his bed.

And then he'd given Median a Red Rocket Pop.

Dinner came shortly after—a tray with Napa cabbage, smashed sweet potatoes with a sprinkle of cinnamon, and baked thyme chicken with hand-squeezed lemon juice to drink, the perfect balance of sweet and tart. The food was really good, and Median scarfed down everything, including the egg custard, which he'd never been a fan of in life.

That turned his appetite. He'd foregone his humanity, his life, consoled by the fact they'd won against evil and that the only woman he'd ever loved was safe. But now, knowing the truth, that he was alive and was only here because Mary had betrayed him, turned his world upside down. Kind of like delicious hospital food—it just was something that wasn't supposed to be.

The day had zipped by, and Median was exhausted. Once he was done with his food and had sneaked to use the restroom one last time alone, he settled into his bed and found himself drifting off.

"There's a big ol' loophole to this place," Thomas T. Telford said.

Median dragged his eyes over to the evil white man standing by the window. The sky was the color of dying embers. Thomas T. Telford was looking outside in the direction of smoke coming from that distant mountain, now the ball of fire had gone out. There were red rivulets covering the landscape, glowing against the darkness. Had he not known he was looking at hell proper, Median thought it might have looked romantic.

"Hell is hell, son. You got to work your own deal. Everything is negotiable."

"Okay," Median replied, not knowing what else to say.

Thomas T. Telford looked at him. Something was off about the old man's eyes. Median dismissed it, though. It wasn't as if he had known him long. There was something off about the whole place and everyone and everything in it. Not the least of which a living human being who was in the what—throat of hell?

"I see you have company," Thomas T. Telford said. "Maybe we'll talk more later."

Median looked to the doorway and saw a nurse—*the nurse*—standing there, the light at her back and her face in shadow, except for those red pupils.

There was a breeze from the window, and Median glanced back, just in time to see Thomas T.

Telford's bare feet upside down before they
disappeared.

"Did he just?"

"Shhhhh," the demon nurse said from inside
the door. She undid the top few buttons of her
uniform, exposing a wealth of pushed-up cleavage.

Median tried to crawl backward into his
mattress when she approached. He didn't want her
to touch him, and at the same time, his body craved
it. If he'd sat down to count, he could have figured
exactly how many women he'd had sex with in his
lifetime, and no matter how physically attractive,
none of them had put it on him the same way this
nurse had with only her hand.

"Do you want me to touch you?" she asked
him.

Median shook his head. "Yes."

Dammit! he thought.

She let her hands roam up and down her
body, squeezing and pulling deliciously. The nurse
approached, and he began to stiffen. She bent over,
giving him two heaping eyeball-scoops of ass. A
moan escaped him, and he pushed his rising hands
back down before he could do who knew what with
those beautiful hills of pants meat.

Her face was still covered in shadow, save
for those eyes, when she faced him again. She came
around and licked him, her silken tongue lashing his
cheek before she continued over his gown, trailing
down to his stomach.

The demon nurse nuzzled his crotch with
her face, and it was all he could do not to cry out.

All the nerves from his thighs to his navel began singing in three-part harmony.

"Do you want me to?" she asked him, her breath flame-hot on his groin. She began dragging his gown up his calf, over his knee...

"Nnnnnno," Median managed to say.

She looked at him with those fire-red pupils.

"Pleeeeeeeease, Walker?" The nurse pinched a nipple through her uniform. "It's the only way I can cum!"

His already jogging heart began sprinting. Median's blood rushed in his ears.

"I...don't consent...to this." The words were like brick-heavy razors coming out of his mouth.

The demon nurse's smile was somehow wider than her face, reminding him he was dreaming. He thought he was getting stronger. Median cleared his throat and found his voice really was his.

"Stop," he said.

She froze, her eyes locked on his.

There was the small sound of rustling fabric. Median didn't know where it was coming from and took his eyes off her long enough to look around the room. The breeze from the window had stopped, and he couldn't see anything else moving.

"Looks like someone wants me to keep going," the nurse said in Dr. Rick's voice.

Median looked down, past her head. The sound was coming from his gown, which seemed to be pulling its way up of its own accord.

Until he saw the movement at his crotch.

"No," he said. "No."

His penis continued flopping back and forth, pulling the gown up on its own until it peeked out from the bottom. The demon nurse's smile was painfully wide. Shiny teeth like glowing rings of triangular daggers lined an infinitely deep, black throat. She turned her head toward his throbbing member, reared back, and—

Median woke up when he came.

It was a distant second to his orgasm on that porn set, when he'd practically been begging for death before it was over, but it was still pretty strong. He could only describe the sound coming involuntarily out of him as howling. His cock pulsed while he painted the crotch of his gown.

Although his eyes were shut in ecstasy, he could hear her parting words in his waking mind.

"I'm gonna pick you up by the scruff of your neck and devour you, cock first. And you're gonna love it."

Was she Dr. Rick? Was that how she was going to eat him at her/his wedding? Median heard a familiar click and opened his eyes, seeing someone at the foot of his bed, holding a camera. Then he felt someone standing almost cheek to cheek with him.

"Wutthefug?" Median said, spent, his mind dragging.

"Let's get one more," the man too close to him said. He wrapped his arm around Median's head, and the camera flashed again.

From the angle where the woman was crouched, she'd definitely nabbed a picture of his soaked, tent-poled gown. Median's first thought was to tell them to give him a moment and take the picture again, but his head—particularly his mouth—was filled with cotton balls.

"Say, what do you say about getting that tour now?" someone said.

Dr. Rick stood in a crowd of men and women by the open door. "Absolutely, Mr. Mayor," he said. "Right this way."

"Any chance we could take my new buddy with us?" The mayor—*whoever he was*—thumbed over his shoulder at Median.

Dr. Rick paused a moment. "Of course."

Median was still recuperating when they got him into his wheelchair. The mayor squeezed in to grab a hold of the handles, getting another photo op before relinquishing to whatever staffer while they visited different areas of the hospital.

Median noticed the bandage on his arm had been changed, and he half absentmindedly scratched at it. A moment later, they were getting on the elevator, and his stomach was rumbling.

"What about breakfast?" Median asked.

"Hey, buddy." The mayor looked down at him and knelt.

Median blinked heavily, forcing his eyes to focus on the man who was suddenly way too close. The mayor pinned a button to Median's gown and said, "Vote Doolot." His breath smelled like Jack Daniels and chili cheese corn chips.

"If he's that excited, maybe he should vote early by absentee ballot," one of the other people in the elevator car said, and the rest of the group laughed.

For a moment of panic, Median thought he might have had another boner, but when he looked, the line of drool coming from his mouth trailed down his gown. He swiped his hand over his mouth, finding the little bit of movement disorienting. Median was still struggling to cobble together his thoughts when they got off the elevator.

They'd drugged him. Was that standard procedure when politicians visited hell?

He didn't care. A lot had happened over the last twenty-four hours, and he hadn't had proper opportunity to explore it. Most significant was the fact he was alive—and the devil planned on eating him at his wedding tomorrow. That was too entirely large for Median to process at the moment, so he moved to the next one.

Mary.

The woman he'd loved—*still loved*—had been the one responsible for him going to hell. She'd betrayed him *twice,* and he'd been foolish enough to trust her after the first time. Well, if he hadn't, he more than likely would have been dead now, but still.

Dr. Rick—the devil himself—stopped by a room here and there in a long corridor and explained what was going on inside when each door opened. At least, that's what Median figured. It took a lot of effort to follow along with the words, and it was a lot easier in his head, crawled up with his own thoughts.

He felt like just giving in. Like there was no reason not to let the devil gobble him up. Hell, he might not have lasted that long anyway, if he had another one of those nightmares with that thing threatening to devour him as soon as it made him cum. If he had another session with Dr. Saranc, he intended to ask her what that was all about.

So, the love of his life hated him. Not much he could do about it, and she definitely wasn't the first person he'd cared about who had nothing but hatred for him in return. He just wished she'd told him. They could have had a conversation—even if he'd wound up in the exact same place he was right now. Median could have digested it better had he just known how she'd felt.

He also thought about Thomas T. Telford. Why the hell had he jumped out the window? And again, just like with Vinny, how come nobody cared? Was it because it was hell and death here was just part of a larger theme?

They came to another door, and when it swung open, what was going on inside caught Median's attention. There was a bald-headed woman in a lab coat, with huge round spectacles and a clipboard in her hands, watching…watching…

Median had to blink several times before he could process what was before his eyes.

A chunky naked man with a bucket hung beneath his neck was on his hands and knees atop a metal examination table. A petite, brown-eyed woman, also naked, sat on a metal stool to the rear and right of the man, holding a tablespoon with the business end coated with what appeared to be mayonnaise.

"Again," the woman with the clipboard said.

"Please..." the man pleaded. His eyes were red-rimmed, a drop of sweat hanging from his nose.

Something sloshed in the bucket hanging around his neck, and Median had no interest in confirming what he thought it was. The brown-eyed woman dipped the spoon, shaking off the excess mayonnaise, before going in the man's ass with it. He grunted when she turned the handle of the spoon up and extracted it—just like feeding a baby—then put it back into the who-knew-how-many gallons of mayonnaise jar on the small table in front of her. It was more than half empty. She pulled out another healthy spoonful and waited.

"Again," the woman with the clipboard demanded.

"That is quite impressive there," Mayor Doolot said to Dr. Rick.

They moved onto the next room, laid out exactly the same as the last, except the test subject was a painfully thin, naked man who had the longest ballsack Median had ever seen. He was thinking the bald woman—who looked just like the other one—was going to do something to his genital area, but instead, she pressed a big black button on the wall. A red strobe light on the ceiling came on, and the man turned to what looked like a small dishwasher that barely came up to his thigh.

The man bent to open the appliance and set about the complicated task of putting himself inside. Median didn't think it was going to be possible.

While the unit was taller than either the man's calf or thigh bone was long, it was too small for an adult to fit in. The man got down on his hands and knees and tried putting in an arm, then his torso. He turned around and backed in with his legs but still wasn't able to fit.

Everyone watched with intense curiosity. He put his head in and tried driving the rest of his body with his bare feet. The man got to his knees and stood, posing with one arm across his stomach and his opposite hand to his mouth, a look of deep concentration on his gaunt face. His long sack almost brushed the floor.

When he turned his back to the unit, he stretched his arms out to his sides and drew his feet together. He sort of looked like he was about to make a complicated dive from a platform, but instead, his thin muscles bulged, and there were several pops. His arms continued flexing backward, his shoulders and elbows and even his *fingers* dislocating. His knees folded behind him with a thicker version of the popping, and he lowered to the floor. His legs neatly filled the inside of the unit to either side, drawing his torso in.

For a moment, Median thought the man would hit his balls on the floor, but he slowed just enough to rest them gently on the linoleum before dragging them and the rest of his body inside.

The whole thing had happened so fast, Median was certain it had to have been practiced and the show of him figuring out what wouldn't work was just for the mayor and the rest of the onlookers. Median couldn't imagine the intensity of

the pain the man must have been in while he smiled,
one hand crawling over his mostly bald head,
grabbing the edge of the door of the unit, and
swinging it closed.

They passed several more rooms, including
one with three apparently dead bodies on what
looked like a makeshift clothes rack. Something like
electrical currents were being passed through them.
One of the bodies swayed gently, and even though
Median didn't see anything special going on, the
bald-headed woman in the lab coat and glasses—
triplets? quintuplets? septuplets?—was writing
furiously, glancing up occasionally.

The last room they came to had a
chimpanzee sitting across a table from a
bewildered-looking Asian woman, showing her
Rorschach cards. It slapped her after every card,
whether she answered or not.

"Well, that was just great," Mayor Doolot
said. "Don't you think so, guys?"

"Absolutely," a slender woman in a business
suit agreed.

The entire group applauded for a moment.
Dr. Rick smiled and dropped his head in humility.

"What do you say we get one more picture?"
Mayor Doolot asked. "All of us, on the front steps
of the building."

"I don't see why not." Dr. Rick looked at
Median for the first time and smiled wide. "We'd be
happy to."

Someone pushed Median's wheelchair, and
they all went back to the elevator, which stood
open, waiting for them. They got on, and Dr. Rick

thumbed a button. The doors slid shut. A moment later, they were on the main floor. It was daylight out, something Median didn't recall seeing before, the one time he was here.

There were patients milling about, some dragging IV poles with clear bags of whatever hooked on them. Nurse Tropos stopped Dr. Rick at the vestibule doors, and they exchanged words. She looked over her shoulder at Median, her mouth a grim line.

He was terrible at reading lips, but he managed to make out her last few words.

Make it quick.

Dr. Rick led the mayor's posse outside, and whoever was pushing Median's wheelchair spun him around to take him down the set of stairs, one bump at a time. Median was sure a hospital was supposed to have a ramp, but he imagined a hospital that was some sort of entryway to hell had to have been a minefield of deficiencies for the ADA.

At the bottom of the stairs, someone locked Median's wheelchair, and the mayor hunched next to him. The rest of his staff spread out behind them, as if they'd practiced this specific maneuver many times over.

It was as bright outside as it was chilly. Median had difficulty believing this was hell. It seemed so much like the real world. The sky was bright blue, save for a few trails of clouds. Cars were driving by in either direction on the street. A woman in black stretch pants, a red puffer vest jacket, and earmuffs jogged by.

Was *this the real world*?

The tips of Median's fingers and toes were tingling along with his lips. Whatever he'd been shot with was wearing off. He tried flexing the muscles of his thighs and found he was able to move them in real time, rather than feeling like he was commanding his body through distant remote control.

If he were alive…and if this were the real world…could he just get up and run? The mayor's security detail was for the mayor. He didn't think they would pursue him if he got up and ran away. And Dr. Rick—satan or no—wasn't physically capable of catching him if Median could break away from the crowd. Median was even willing to risk getting clipped by a car. He hardly believed Dr. Rick would go full devil in the middle of the day in whatever Detroit suburb this was.

Median's heart was racing. He began minor tests of the muscles of his legs and back, lifting his foot a micro-inch, flexing his spine. Everything felt like it was working the way it was supposed to. Maybe he'd stumble, but as long as he didn't fall, that could work in his favor. Maybe someone would reach for him, grab a hold of his gown. But the thin material would either tear or the whole thing would come off his body. Median didn't care if he had to run down Palmer Road naked in the cold, so long as he was escaping hell.

Wait, he *did* recognize where he was. This was Westland…or Inkster. One of those. He hadn't been to this area often, but enough times that where he was finally hit him. It was all he could do not to spring out of this wheelchair right then and start hoofing it.

One of the mayor's staffers stood in front of the group with his smartphone—a muscular, bald-headed short man with no eyebrows. Everyone pulled in tight.

And then Dr. Rick was on Median's other side, putting a hand on his shoulder.

"Everyone say 'cheese'!" the man holding the phone said.

Median felt himself freeze—literally freeze—ice filling his veins, his face paralyzed, and his arms and legs stiff as tree limbs.

The man lowered the smartphone and said, "All right, my turn!"

But the group broke up.

"Hey, guys, what about me?"

Mayor Doolot straightened and shook Dr. Rick's hand. "Thanks for having us, doctor," he said with a smile as wide as the devil's. "I'm very impressed. Looking forward to seeing what comes from your research and your continued partnership with the city."

Research? Median thought. As far as he understood, the main purpose of St. Elo was reeducating the dead so they could more effectively appreciate the torments of hell. Research was a whole other thing. As if the place *needed* more reason to be sinister.

Someone began wheeling Median backward toward the stairs, and he realized his moment was quickly evaporating. The wheelchair stopped a moment, then they began the slow process of bumping back up the steps.

"You always assume what's in front of your eyes is real," the devil whispered in Median's ear. "Everything you touch, everything you smell, everything you taste is just god's imagination plucking away at your strings. *I* won't lie to you. I just want to yank away the whole facade and show you the terrible, terrible underneath." He licked Median's earlobe. "You'll be so excited, you'll never stop screaming."

Median heard the words but was slow in processing them. There were several other wheels already turning in his mind. Mainly, the beginning of how he would get his revenge. He wouldn't destroy hell. No, he didn't want a bunch of errant evil souls running around. Something that would be an inconvenience. Something that would make the devil curse his name whenever he thought of Median.

And he also wondered, *Where did they get all that mayo?*

Chapter 14. My God, My Boyfriend

"A *god*?" Mary asked. "What do you mean, you're a god?"

"Please," Derek said, looking around. "Not so loud."

Mary had left the building in a huff, feeling like she was smuggling a bowling ball under her dress. The baby was pressing on her bladder, and she needed to take a pee, but she had no intention of setting foot in that building again.

"*You're a god, Derek*!" Mary yelled when she opened her car door. Derek had tried to open it, but she'd slapped his hand away. "You didn't think I needed to know that?"

"I...No...I mean, yes." Derek circled the car to the passenger side. "I didn't know how to tell you."

"Which one?" Mary got in and started the engine.

"Huh?" he asked, stuffing himself inside.

The tires chirped when she pulled away.

"Which god? Which god are you? Are you Zeus or something?"

"No." Derek scoffed. "I am not Zeus. I'm me. I'm Derek."

"But you're a god. A *god,* Derek."

"Okay, I'm actually a demi-god. I have to die to become a full god."

Mary bore into him with her stare, her eyes leaving the road for at least five seconds. That was hardly the point, and she wanted him to know that.

Derek reached for the steering wheel, paused, and put his hand back in his lap.

"Okay, my father…you probably haven't heard of him."

"What's his name?"

"Agé."

"And I suppose he was a dick and abandoned you like gods do, right?"

"No." Derek made a face. "That's actually an offensive stereotype. I mean, for any of the gods outside of the Greek and Roman pantheons. We have a pretty good relationship. We call each other every week."

"You know what, you're right. You're right. I'm sorry for that. *He's* not the dick right now." Mary found herself calming down, which was pissing her off. Derek had that damn calming effect on her, and now she couldn't help but think it was by some supernatural means, intentional or not. She could understand why a demi-god who just wanted to live a normal life might not want the world to know…

—But dammit, he should have told *her*!

"What can you do?" she asked Derek. "Like powers or whatever?"

Derek shrugged his big shoulders. "I dunno. I'm strong. I'm a pretty good hunter, but well, y'know, I'm a vegan, so…"

"You don't shoot lightning out of your fingers? Thunder out of your ass?"

"Okay, you're being sarcastic. You about ready to forgive me?"

Shit, she was. Mary had been driving around aimlessly, not wanting to go home, but too anxious to sit still. They were somewhere on the east side, but that was the extent of what she could tell.

Mary pulled over to the curb next to a boarded-up gas station.

"I need you to get out," she said.

"What?" Derek sat up in his seat. He looked around. "Here? But I left my truck—"

"I really need to sort things out right now. I'm about to have a baby, and…and I just really need to think."

He stared at her for a long time while she forced her eyes to remain on the steering wheel. Then Derek unpacked himself from the little car and gently closed the door. He turned and stooped to look at her through the window. She rolled it up on him, forcing him to step back.

Derek was just so big. Rolling the window up shouldn't have had any kind of finality to it, considering he looked like he could just heft the little car up on his shoulder with her in it.

"I am sorry, Mary." He looked sadder than she'd ever seen him.

She flashed a smile before quickly looking away. "I know, Derek."

Chapter 15. The Fountain of Useless Knowledge

They wandered for what felt like hours. Alfred had no idea how to tell the passage of time. There were no clocks in the city, and the sun was always in the same position in the annoyingly blue, obnoxiously cloudless sky.

The angels seemed to be all gone, headed to whatever battle. And he'd been right in his initial estimation of the populace here—everyone was an idiot. The first person he'd encountered en route to find this Morgan was a naked woman in the middle of the golden cobblestone street, munching on her own tunic.

"Could you tell us how to find Morgan?" he'd asked her, even though he suspected he wouldn't get any sort of an intelligible answer.

She'd rolled her big hazel eyes on him, and save for the long trail of drool hanging from her mouth, he supposed she was probably one of the most beautiful people he'd ever seen. When he thought about it, even the old man, Atta, had been handsome.

"Morgan," she'd said and laughed. "Morgan-Morgan-Morgan-Morgan." Her eyes drifted away from him and settled on some distant point while she'd repeated his name.

"The streets hold their secrets, like lovers in the night," Hammercock said.

Alfred looked at him.

The old man knew Alfred hated when he spoke like that. "Sorry."

Alfred was amazed he felt no hunger, no exhaustion, after they'd walked so long. There was a stone fountain along the side of the road when they rounded a corner. Solely out of habit, he decided to have a drink.

"Sir! Excuse me, sir!" someone called to him just before Alfred bent to take a sip.

Alfred glanced at the man, who looked like the stereotypical version of god. Big bushy white beard and a head of unruly hair, laser-sharp blue eyes. The man was handsome too.

"I'd suggest not drinking from *that* fountain."

"What, is it a 'Whites Only' drinking fountain?" Alfred asked the old white man.

He looked curiously at Alfred, as if he wanted to ask what he meant. "I don't know about that, but that's a Fountain of Pointless Knowledge. If you have a thirst to learn, you'll crave more the more you drink. It's only good for a swig when you're bored at parties and need something to talk about."

"What?" That didn't make sense to Alfred, and he dismissed the man by turning his back on him.

Alfred took a sip. The water tasted cleaner than any he'd ever had, to the point of almost being sweet. It cooled his entire body, though he hadn't been hot before, and he began gulping it down as quickly as it filled his mouth.

Every time you lick a stamp, you consume one-tenth of a calorie...

Alfred stood from the fountain, unsure where the thought had come from. The coolness coursing through him immediately left, and his mouth felt dry. He drank more, the sensation filling him once again.

A pig's orgasm lasts for thirty minutes...

The more he filled his stomach with the water, the more he craved.

Mel Blanc was allergic to carrots...

More people are killed annually by donkeys than plane crashes...

Barbie's full name is Barbara Millicent Roberts...

For a brief moment of panic, Alfred realized all this new information was crowding out things he'd already known. Farewell went the Aramaic alphabet and the anatomy of the pygmy marmoset. He tried to push away but somehow wound up pulling his entire face into the fountain, the water flooding into his eyes, nose, and mouth.

Reindeer like to eat bananas...

The human stomach has to produce a new layer of mucus every two weeks, or it will digest itself...

Most American car horns honk in the key of F...

A jiffy is a unit of time of one-one hundredth of a second.

Hammercock pulled him back, but he wanted to thrust his face into the water to drink more. "Angel! Angel, stop!" he said. "You're drowning!"

It was all Alfred could do to just stand still. He wanted the water, needed it. But the well of hatred within him was rooted deeper than the water could reach. Second by second, he felt more himself, until he was able to take a step back.

"The old man," Alfred said to Hammercock. "The one who tried to warn me about the fountain. Get him."

Hammercock nodded and walked toward where they'd seen him. Alfred could still feel the water's pull, but he was able to resist, taking another step back before something moved beneath his sandaled foot.

"Sir! Excuse me, sir!"

The man appeared right in front of Hammercock. He was about the same height as Alfred, and Hammercock tried and failed to grab him, his hands passing harmlessly through.

"I'd suggest not drinking from *that* fountain," the man said.

Alfred looked down. One of the golden cobblestones was different from the others. He stepped on it again.

"Sir! Excuse me, sir!" The white-haired man appeared again.

"What are you?" Alfred asked. "Some sort of A.I. or a programmed message on a loop?"

The bearded man looked at him, confused, and said, "I don't know what you're talking about."

"Sure, you do. On *some* level." Alfred didn't approach, knowing it was a sort of hologram, considering Hammercock had tried and failed to touch it. He looked around to see if he could determine if it were being projected from one of the buildings. "You're able to vary your answers, so you know *something*."

The figure held up a finger. "My only intent is to warn you about the Fountain of Pointless Knowledge. Don't drink from it."

"I already did."

The bearded man cocked his head to one side.

"Really?" Then he vanished.

Alfred stepped on the plate again.

"Sir! Excuse me, sir!" The white-haired man appeared again.

It was about a twenty-two second loop, by Alfred's count. Hammercock stood by, confused.

"What other fountains are there?" Alfred asked.

"There are Fountains of Pointless Knowledge all about the city," the old man said.

"What is the point of the fountains?"

The man looked confused. "Why, to know god."

"What is the nature of god?"

The man shook his head as if he hadn't understood Alfred's question. Alfred stepped on the plate again. A twin of the old man appeared a foot away from the first, and they looked at each other.

"Sir! Excuse me—" the second one began.

"Who are you?" Alfred asked.

"I—uhh."

The first one disappeared. Alfred stepped on the plate again.

"Sir!" A new one appeared.

Alfred stepped on the plate several times. Five more bearded old men appeared. They were about to speak but then noticed one another.

"What is your purpose?" Alfred asked.

"To warn you about the peril of the Fountain of Pointless Knowledge," they said in unison.

"Okay, I won't drink from it, then. Are there other fountains with useful knowledge?"

All six figures began to vibrate. Alfred stepped on the plate two more times, but no more of them appeared. They all stood up straight, their faces going blank. One by one, they slid into each other until there was only one left.

"You seek the Fountain of Knowledge," the single bearded man said. Alfred noted he had an actual intelligence behind his eyes. He walked toward Alfred. "Why would you want such a thing? You are in heaven. You could have anything you can imagine."

"I want *knowledge*," Alfred replied.

"True Knowledge is dangerous," he said, pronouncing the "K" in *knowledge* for some reason: Kuh-nowledge. "Why court such a thing in a world where anything could be yours?" He spread his arms.

Hammercock must have sensed his master was in danger and stepped in front of the old man. Without breaking eye contact with Alfred, the bearded old man placed a hand on Hammercock's shoulder, forcing him to his knees instantly. Hammercock tried to break his grasp, but it was like a toddler trying to fight off an adult. The man shoved Hammercock to the ground and stood before Alfred.

"Knowledge only belongs to the true one. The first."

"And who is that?" Alfred stood nose-to-nose with the white-haired man. "Is it Morgan?"

Something flashed in the man's eyes, and that was all Alfred needed for confirmation. The bearded man raised a hand to strike him down, and Alfred waited until the downstroke of his blow to step aside and yank him by his robes, using his forward momentum to propel him into the Fountain of Pointless Knowledge. The man struck the fountain, shattering it, and a flood of water blasted him in the face when he fell to his knees.

He tried to stand, but he was either stuck where he was or the effect of the water worked on him too. His mouth stretched open impossibly wide, and he guzzled the torrent of water. His body flashed with blue light, as if he were fighting and losing against the effects of the water.

"How did you know that would work?" Hammercock asked him.

"I didn't." Alfred adjusted his tunic and started walking. "I was just guessing. But the one thing I'm sure of is, I need to find this Morgan character. I think he might be tied into why everyone here is so…stupid."

Chapter 16. About Last Night

Lunch was lemon honey-roasted shrimp with fettuccine and some sort of Italian soda, which was lemon and mint flavored. Median devoured everything and had a vegan chocolate chip cupcake sweetened with beets. *Beets.* This might have been hell, but the eating was Michelin approved.

An orderly came shortly after he'd finished and traded his empty tray for another Red Rocket Pop. He hadn't really wanted it but unwrapped and began eating it anyway.

"I woke up in a dumpster, wearing nothing but a pair of red bottoms, spooning a prosthetic leg," Thomas T. Telford said, being wheeled into the room by that same tall nurse as yesterday. "Needless to say, that was the last time they let me babysit." He cackled, and she parked the wheelchair by his bed to help him up.

Median stared in amazement. He *had* seen the old man take a header out of the window, hadn't he? He hadn't exactly been paying attention when he woke up this morning, but he was pretty sure Thomas T. Telford hadn't been in here.

Because he'd jumped out the window. Right?

The old man stood, grunting. He swung his legs into bed, and the nurse covered him up to his chest with a thin hospital blanket. She nodded to Median on her way out.

"Where's my clicker?" Thomas T. Telford asked.

Median watched the man fish it up from the side of the bed by the cord. The flatscreen on the opposite side of the room flashed on, and a moment later, Thomas T. Telford was flipping through channels.

"Ooo, *A Different World.*"

Median remembered watching the spinoff of *The Cosby Show* when he was a preteen. It was more of a staple in his household than a show he'd actually found funny. He didn't recognize this particular episode, but his mind drifted to Lisa Bonet and how she'd left the show, then how Dwyane Wayne and Whitley Gilbert had been established as love interests. It had been high drama at the time when Dwayne went to her wedding and professed his love for her. Median was a little bit older when he realized how much of a trope breaking up a wedding on the wedding day was. Hadn't they done that on *Cheers* too?

Thomas T. Telford continued flipping through the channels, not finding anything satisfactory, until he'd gone through all of them. Median started recognizing some of the programs. Thomas T. Telford finally settled on a gameshow—*Press Your Luck.* The host welcomed the viewing public back from the commercial and began addressing the three contestants.

"Hey, Mr. Telford?" Median said.

"What's that, son?" Thomas T. Telford lowered the volume.

"Could I ask…Was last night real?"

"Real as in, did I…" He walked his index and middle fingers like legs across one thigh and let the hand plummet over the side of the bed.

"But…how are you here?"

Thomas T. Telford smiled. "You're asking the wrong question. Now, if you'd asked me 'why', I might be inclined to tell you, in all my years walking planet Earth, I never found a loophole I wouldn't take if it got me what I wanted. That"—he pointed to the window—"is my loophole."

"You look fine, though."

"Thank you. Not bad for an old man who's been dead nine years."

"That's right. You can't die in hell. You're already dead."

"I wouldn't go that far. It is possible for a soul to be destroyed. It's just hard to do."

"Is that what you're trying to do?" Median asked.

"Nope. I was working the mines in New Be'er Shachat and one day got the bright idea to throw myself in a molten pit. Shit, that hurt. Well, that was by far worse than my actual punishment—at least, *they* thought—so they sent me here to recuperate."

"Is that why you jumped out the window?"

"Not jumped, son. Jump. I do it every night. I'll take a little bit of pain rather than going back to manual labor. You see how they feed us here, right?"

"So they're trying to get you right in the head so they can torture you again. But what you're doing is worse than your punishment. How do they not catch on?"

"Look at this place," Thomas T. Telford said. "I mean, *really* look at it. The inmates are running the asylum here. There are very few qualified professionals in this place. The only thing anyone around here knows to do is keep a routine."

"You know Dr. Rick is the devil, right?"

Thomas T. Telford laughed. "He's probably the most incompetent of all of them. I met him once. The guy's an idiot. I can't stress how overwhelmingly stupid he is. I guess being a complete imbecile is a qualification to run things around here. It's a shame he's got that fine piece of a nurse wants to marry him. What a waste."

"They're gonna eat me tomorrow," Median said. A trickle of red juice trailed down his thumb, and he licked it off. He didn't feel like finishing the pop and put it on one of the machines lying dormant beside him.

"Excuse me?"

"Tomorrow. At some point during the wedding ceremony, they're going to eat me."

"Why would they do that?"

"I'm alive. I think it might be some sort of ritual. I don't know."

"You're good with this?"

"It's not like I have a choice in the matter. I had a plan to escape, but the demon that was helping me got skinned."

"You could always try the old window method. See how that works out for ya."

"No. I mean, I'd rather kill myself than get eaten, but I just can't bring myself to do anything like that."

"I could do it for you." Thomas T. Telford made a shoving motion with both hands. "Really quick. You'd never see it coming."

Median shook his head. "Thanks, but no. I mean, if I agreed to that, I wouldn't be able to turn my back on you."

Thomas T. Telford nodded. "Yeah, I getcha. Say, I missed lunch. Wanna come to the cafeteria with me?"

"Why not?"

Both men got in their wheelchairs and rolled out of the room. They took the elevator down. The guard who'd been there yesterday was gone. Maybe he was on a break.

They wheeled off the elevator and past the concierge desk just inside St. Eloise's main entrance. Median had gone through these very doors not more than an hour ago, but what was out there now was definitely not what he'd seen earlier.

The skyline was still burning in the distance, casting varying shades of red across the landscape and sky. He wondered if outside had just been some sort of optical illusion. But wouldn't that have meant Mayor Doolot had come to hell?

Median didn't understand how this hospital could be in two places at once, but that must have been the case. Unless it could move back and forth. But if *that* were the case, wouldn't a building appearing and disappearing in the real world get noticed?

He followed Thomas T. Telford into the cafeteria. His mind drifted away from thoughts of escape when the smell wafting from the kitchen filled his nose. Thomas T. Telford got cheesy smothered mushroom chicken with a side of baked glazed carrots. Median was still full from lunch, but a slice of red velvet cake caught his eye.

They took their food to a round table, pushing away two of the chairs to make room for their wheelchairs.

"I don't know what to tell you, son," Thomas T. Telford said, digging in after he'd cut his chicken into bite-sized cubes. "Idiots or no, they are efficient prison guards. I don't see how you get out. You know, I saw this documentary once. It was about a guy—a serial killer—who'd been caught by his estranged son and put on death row. Before they took him for execution, he had a television in his cell, and he'd rigged it to give himself some sort of electric shock. Stopped his heart cold.

"So the guards come get him to sit in Ol' Sparky's lap, and they find him dead. One of the guards gives him mouth-to-mouth, and you know what he did?"

"He bites the guard's lip," Median said. "I saw *Shocker* too."

"*Shocker*?" Thomas T. Telford asked. "What's that?"

"It's a movie. You're describing the scene when they were about to electrocute Horace Pinker."

"Well, that was his name, but it wasn't a movie. It was a two-part documentary. I saw it on *Dateline* or *20/20*. One of those."

"Down here?"

Thomas T. Telford nodded. Rather than arguing any further, Median realized reality and fiction from the living world might blend together in some kind of way in hell. Maybe it *was* a documentary.

"Mind if I sit here?"

Both men looked up at the pretty blonde with glasses and a lab coat on, placing her tray down.

It was *her*.

"There's always room for a pretty lady." Thomas T. Telford held out a hand for her to sit.

She looked between the two men and smiled at them both.

"I'm Beatricia," she said.

"Yes, you are." Median mentally kicked himself for saying something so banal. "I-I'm—"

"Walker Harris," she said for him. "And you are Thomas T. Telford."

"I see our reputations precede us," Thomas T. Telford replied.

And that's when the thought hatched in Median's mind, fully formed. Well, not exactly *how* he was going to do it, but *what* he was going to do. Maybe he could piss the devil off enough he'd just kill him outright instead of eating him.

"So…I hear you're getting married tomorrow?" Median asked.

"Oh, yeah." She smiled. "I can't wait."

"How long have you known Dr. Rick?"

"I met him earlier this year," she said. "Not long after I started working here."

Median found himself measuring what he wanted to say. He knew she, too, was alive and had a feeling there were other staff members here who were, but how much they knew was another story. Median couldn't just outright say her fiancé was satan.

"Was there a lot of planning for the wedding?"

Beatricia shook her head and forked spaghetti into her mouth. "Dr. Rick took care of all of it. I mean, getting married at St. Elo isn't ideal, but the chapel is actually really nice."

"Why *are* you getting married here?" Median asked. "I mean, there's a lot of places you could go. I always wanted to get married at the Detroit Zoo."

"Yeah, they *do* do weddings there, don't they?"

"A hospital's just as good as any place, I say," Thomas T. Telford said. "'Cept for my last one, I had a big to-do in a church, tons of guests, all the pomp and circumstance you could ask for." Thomas T. Telford speared a cube of chicken with his fork and pointed it at Median. "Now the Vegas one, that's the one that stuck."

The old man was stepping all over the only angle Median had been able to think of so far. "Didn't you say your wife killed you?" Median asked him.

"My last *three* wives, thank you," Thomas T. Telford said, munching on a mouthful of chicken. He had a little twinkle in his eye, like it was a point of pride.

"So…where are you going to go after the wedding? Hawaii? Italy? Montana?"

"No." Beatricia sighed. "Dr. Rick can't get any time off. He barely will have enough time for the wedding."

Well, at least *that* was a feather in Median's cap for the marriage's likelihood of failing. Too bad being eaten was part of the ceremony; otherwise, he might like his chances for the rebound guy.

"Say, are you guys doing anything—I dunno—*special* for the wedding?"

"What do you mean?"

"I know sometimes people have certain things in their culture they like to honor during a wedding ceremony. You know, jumping the broom or stepping on a wine glass—stuff like that."

"Actually, yes. I mean, I don't know what it is, but Dr. Rick's grandmother on his father's side is Icelandic or something, and he wants to incorporate something they do into the wedding."

"What's that?"

"I don't know. He said it's a surprise."

Median had a pretty good idea of what, but he didn't think he could just blurt out her fiancé was intending to devour him. "You don't want to know?" he asked.

"Sure, I do," she said. "But that's Dr. Rick. He's always so full of surprises."

She went all dreamy-eyed, and it was all Median could do to keep from punching his slice of rich, moist, decadent red velvet cake. Instead, he cut a big chunk with his fork, speared it, and shoveled it into his mouth.

Thomas T. Telford must have seen something in Median's eyes because he jumped in again. "You know what I say? Take your time. Y'know, don't rush into anything like having kids or anything. Make sure you get all that energy out on each other first, if you know what I'm saying."

Beatricia's cheeks turned red. Median's whole head felt hot.

"Y'know, it was a good ten years before me and the first missus had our first. I mean, I had two before *we* had any, but the point is, we got everything out our systems we needed to first."

"You know, we haven't even talked about having children," she said.

"You think you want any?" Median managed to ask. "I bet you'd be a great mom. I mean, that's a really big step, and I'm sure you don't want to be on opposite ends."

"I guess," Beatricia said. "I have a niece and a nephew. I'm their favorite auntie, but then again, I'm their *only* auntie. I don't think it matters. Whenever I'm with Rick, I feel like we're gonna take over the world."

Median ate his cake in silence, trying to swallow the sting of her last sentence and think of a way to steer the conversation back to when he'd first seen her. But he realized he couldn't exactly do that now. Here she was, gushing about her soon-to-

127

be husband…How was he going to bring up seeing her shoot a double penetration scene?

Median wanted desperately to say something, but the words to convince her to leave the devil and run away with him just weren't coming. They all sat in silence, eating, until her pager went off.

"Crap!" she said around a mouthful of food when she looked at it on her hip. "I gotta go." She stood up, hesitating for a moment.

Median felt his moment swirling the drain.

"Um, could you guys take care of this for me?"

"Certainly," Thomas T. Telford said.

Median was so dumbfounded with desperately having nothing to say, he was only able to manage a single nod.

"Thanks." Beatricia left the cafeteria, headed toward the emergency entrance.

Median had watched her go, and he looked back to see Thomas T. Telford picking up where she'd left off with her spaghetti.

"What?" the old man said.

Median shrugged. And started digging in with his own fork.

It had zucchini in it. *Zucchini*!

Chapter 17. Hunger

This shit *hurt.*

Mary sat as still as possible while a massive contraction squeezed her like an underripe zit. She felt like she'd been stuffed with a watermelon.

The tremendous guilt she felt for making Derek get out of the car was eased when she reminded herself he was a god, but then, had he been a normal person, she might have just left him in a potentially dangerous part of the city…But then she reminded herself none of it would have happened had he not lied to her…But then, was it so unreasonable to not lead with that information, especially considering she hadn't told him her husband was a pornstar, even though they weren't together anymore…

The whole cycle made her incredibly hungry. Mary had stopped by a White Castle drive-thru for a sack of twenty and was polishing off the last one before she pulled into her driveway.

She was starving by the time she got through the front door. And she had to pee. Mary grabbed leftover pizza and salad from the fridge and waddled as quickly as she could to the toilet. It was real bottom-of-the-barrel shit. She sat and began eating.

Mary peed while she ate, something she never imagined she'd do. She went so long she felt like she had to go immediately after she was done and wound up eating the rest of the family-size salad and five slices of pizza before she got up.

Damn, had her belly gotten even bigger?

After she'd washed her hands, Mary looked at the powder room doorway and wasn't sure if it was wide enough to fit through. Her stomach groaned, a low, long, whale-like sound echoing throughout the house. She was hungry again, and when she started digging through the fridge, she made short work of everything prepared, including a half sweet potato pie, two boiled eggs, and rice pudding.

Mary went back in for the sandwich meat and Miracle Whip, grabbing the bread from the top of the fridge. She'd snatched a plate from the cupboard and was about to make sandwiches, but she was so *hungry* again she just took a pile of meat from the package and stuffed her mouth with corned beef. A fistful of bread slices followed, and for just a moment, she had a sensation akin to being choked before realizing it was just the bread getting stuck in her throat.

Mary tried digging out the ball of white bread lodged in there with her index and middle fingers, managing to only extract a six-inch length of crust.

Her stomach felt like it was on fire, and food was the only thing that could put out the flames. She turned on the kitchen sink and grabbed the spray nozzle, intent on blasting the glob down her esophagus. But that only succeeded in turning the dry glob into a pasty ball. Mary tried breathing, wishing she'd been able to learn something from that Lamaze class to calm down. She needed to think this through logically.

Maybe she could Heimlich herself.

Mary looked down at her gigantic belly. No, that wouldn't work. She'd gotten even bigger in the last few minutes. Her whole body felt like it was on fire. Mary needed to feed this baby because it was going to take its nourishment directly out of her if she didn't.

She yanked open the utensil drawer and took out a butterknife. This had to be quick, but she couldn't rush. Butterknife or no, jamming a piece of metal into soft tissue would be bad. Mary stood at her kitchen island, opening her mouth as wide as possible. She took the butterknife delicately by the handle between the index and thumbs of both hands and put the business end into her mouth. Mary rolled her eyes up in her head, not wanting to see any of her gory work, and slowly...slowly reached.

It was like her mouth was a gigantic cave. Mary felt a millisecond of panic, the knife feeling slick between her fingertips, but she was able to keep herself from squeezing, for fear it would squirt out of her grasp and crack a tooth.

Finally, the knife pressed on something. It didn't hurt, so she figured it had to be the bread. Breaking it up would have been ideal, but it was now a gluey ball, and she doubted she had the proper instrumentation to pull that off. A voice in the back of her mind told her to take the knife out of her mouth and call 911, but she silenced it by pointing out she would be dead of starvation before the ambulance got here if she did nothing.

This baby was *eating* her.

The thought alit a sense of urgency, making her jab into the bread and press hard. Something in her throat *clicked*, but she felt it move. It was all she could do to not pump her fist in the air. She carefully withdrew the butterknife and tossed it in the sink.

It wasn't going down easily, but she'd started the work. Mary took a half-empty bottle of Smart Balance cooking oil, screwed off the cap, and turned it upside down, chugging it. She only managed two gulps before the foreign sense of fullness invaded her chest, along with a robust, warm saturation filling her mouth and slowly draining down her esophagus.

Mary stood completely still and waited. Then the bread began moving. She followed up with the rest of the bottle of cooking oil and thought she could hear the sound of sizzling coming from her mouth, like she'd eaten a couple of handfuls of Pop Rocks. Mary dropped the bottle and went back to the refrigerator. She took out the eggs and milk, setting one carton down and opening up the other.

Mary stared at the first egg, and it was almost as if she didn't recognize it. It was as if she were being pushed off the edge of what it meant to be here, to feed this *life* inside her. Eating this raw egg would change her. For the briefest of moments, she thought about maintaining some sense of will.

And then she downed it. Shell and all.

It didn't even crack when she swallowed it. Maybe she'd stretched out her throat already. Maybe the first one had been luck. Before she ate the next one, she took a big gulp of milk.

Mary pounded the next egg. She continued alternating between the two until the milk was gone.

Then she began scooping Miracle Whip into her mouth with three fingers and placing an egg atop the gelatinous mass before swallowing it down.

"Good flavor combo," Mary said at some point before she finished off the fifteen eggs left in the carton.

When the fridge was finally empty, she turned to the freezer. She threw Derek's hot sausages into the microwave and pressed buttons until it started. Something brown had leaked and frozen inside the freezer, and Mary pried up a shard of it, crunching it down without thinking about what she was eating. She grabbed her pint of black cherry ice cream and got frustrated she wasn't able to dig it up with her bare hand. Mary reduced herself to picking up a spoon but became even more aggravated when it bent.

The electronic smell of burning meat filled her nose, and she smashed the carton on the floor, dislodging the fat plug of ice cream. Without a second thought, she got on her hands and knees and devoured it.

The microwave beeped. Mary used the counter to climb to her feet and yanked the door open, seizing one of the sizzling fat sausages and biting it in half. It scalded her mouth, but it was down her throat a second later, the next half following quickly after.

She went on eating out of the microwave with no regard to flavor or what the spicy meat would do to her insides later. Nothing was hotter than the fire filling her right now, and she was desperate to put it out.

Mary came to on the floor. The contraction was like a giant vise on her middle. She groaned, curling into a fetal ball, waiting for what felt like hours before it passed. Mary opened her eyes, and dashes of colors danced in her vision in the dark.

She assumed she must have been out for hours, but when she tried to sit up, she hit her head on something hard.

"Ouch! Shit!" Mary felt around. Whatever she was in, it was cold and metal. Some kind of box. She stretched her legs and was surprised when they didn't meet against whatever she was in. Mary put her feet down and heard the familiar clap of her shoes on her kitchen tile.

Opposing thoughts ran simultaneously through her mind: *What the hell?* and *Oh yeah.*

Mary realized she was headfirst in her oven. She backed out carefully, seeing she had crushed the racks beneath her burgeoning girth. Mary was definitely bigger now but still easily fit in the industrial-sized appliance.

She ignored as best she could the very Plathian implication of her head being in the oven.

Mary had to get back down to St. Eloise. But first she had a craving for some more of that Miracle Whip. And dirt.

Yeah. That would be a *really* good combo.

Chapter 18. Meatus

Morgan had been easy enough to find. And just as disappointing. Alfred had expected someone kingly. Or at least unique. The only thing apparently extraordinary was perhaps him being even dumber than everyone else Alfred had met so far. Hammercock was probably easily smarter than anyone he'd met here.

Morgan was bare-chested, his tunic loosely tied around his waist. And just the same as everyone else, he was physically perfect, barrel-chested, long auburn hair, deep brown eyes, and, well, the tunic could only cover so much and there was certainly *plenty* to cover.

The only old person Alfred had actually seen was the man with the fruit. It was almost as if the residents had designed or redesigned themselves. And then…they'd been turned into idiots? He didn't understand that part. Why were fountains like those even here?

It was almost as if this place held a secret. Despite his disdain for the place, Alfred refused to believe this was all there was to heaven. There had to be more than indifferent or would-be rapist angels and morons who had somehow threaded the eye of the needle.

Morgan had found them rather than the other way around, and for a brief period, Alfred thought there might be some promise in the man. But conversation with him had been a rapid disappointment, with Morgan determined to show his "poopyhole" until Alfred finally just let the man turn around and grab his ankles.

"Th-that's a very nice butthole," Alfred said. "Can you tell us anything about this place?"

"Heaven?" Morgan said, smiling. "We're in heaven."

"That's right. We are." Alfred couldn't help the disgust at the singsong tone reflexively creeping into his voice. "But do you know any more?"

Morgan stared at them without blinking for a long moment. It was oddly unsettling.

"You want I should beat it out of him, Angel?" Hammercock asked.

"No," Alfred said, annoyed.

Even more annoyed that he understood why Hammercock had asked…He was a hammer in constant search of a nail and wanted nothing more than to please his master. Understanding people and being understanding of people had always been two separate things for Alfred; he'd prided himself on the former and had no care for the latter. But either this place or that water was having more of an effect on him than he'd guessed.

"Angel?" Morgan asked. He was a good foot shorter than Alfred, and Alfred allowed him to approach.

Morgan examined him, getting eye level with his jawline, staring intently while he poked the side of Alfred's neck with his middle finger. He felt Alfred's pectorals first over his tunic, and then he slid his hands beneath, massaging them sensually.

Alfred slapped Morgan's hands away, and the shorter man grabbed him by the crotch.

"You like?"

Alfred had never been treated like such a…piece of meat. He restrained himself from throttling Morgan, taking care to remove his hand before stepping back.

"That was…nice," Alfred said, holding a warning hand to Hammercock's chest.

He could clearly see rage on the older man's face and knew Hammercock felt a degree of propriety over him, but Alfred thought he could still make use of Morgan. Beating him to a pulp right now would be counterproductive.

"Could you show me…fun?" Alfred didn't know how to ask what he wanted. He gestured all around, hoping the man would get the hint to take him somewhere interesting.

Instead, he had to stop Morgan from bending over again.

"Not that kind of fun." Alfred wondered how often the angels had taken advantage of him and maybe all the idiots here. If there was any reason to hate the angels, this was it. He grabbed Morgan by the shoulders and stared into his eyes. "Can you take us somewhere fun? A place where people…" Alfred struggled for the words to finish his sentence and looked at Hammercock.

"Go to live," the older man said.

Alfred looked at him quizzically, and he shrugged.

"I was just riffing," Hammercock said.

Alfred was mentally preparing to approach Morgan again, but when he turned to him, the other man was already walking away. Hammercock looked at Alfred, confused, then both hustled to catch up.

Morgan walked in zigzag lines. He climbed through windows and shuffled through buildings with other people in them, who just stared while the three of them walked by. They went into basements and onto roofs, through alleyways, until Alfred was certain he couldn't have figured his way back to where they'd started.

The three of them passed a sign Alfred recognized. Goode Co. had been a maker of snacks based out of Detroit. He wasn't entirely sure if it was still around or not, but seeing the sign brought back memories of snack cakes and potato chips. How odd such a thing would be in heaven.

Finally, they crested a hill that must have been outside of the city proper. Its thin road was only dirt. Alfred walked carefully down the decline, but Morgan rolled and laughed on his way down.

"Ugh." Alfred shook his head in further disgust, only to have Hammercock pass him, rolling down as well.

By the time he reached the bottom, the other two were gathering near a pond. At first, Alfred thought the light was just hitting the water at a strange angle, but no, this wasn't water. It was egg-white with iridescent swirling patterns dancing on the surface with a life of their own.

Morgan waited for him to approach, then pointed. "Soup of Life," he said.

"Soup of Life?" Alfred asked. "What do you mean?"

Morgan put his hands together in front of his face and fluttered his fingertips. The gesture made leaps and bounds toward making him look semi-intellectual. If Alfred had to guess by the stitch in his brow and the tight line of his lips, he was concentrating.

"Make souls for…babies."

"Souls?" Alfred looked at the pond, then back to him. "Souls." He realized with all that water he'd had to drink, he hadn't relieved himself yet. Alfred figured this was the perfect time. What better way to send off new life than with a little bit of pee?

He took his penis out, a grand smile on his face, took a step closer, and aimed.

"Uhh," Hammercock said, covering his mouth.

Good. Let him be abhorred. Alfred welcomed it. Finally, a step in the right direction. Sometimes, when he hadn't gone in a while, it took a moment to pop the seal, so he sighed, waiting patiently. After nothing happened for a full minute, Alfred imagined clenching his sphincter muscles and squeezing his bladder. To be honest, he didn't really feel like he needed to go, but that had been a lot of water.

"Angel?" Hammercock said.

"Shh!" Alfred replied. "It's bad enough I have an audience. I don't need commentators too."

"But…"

"I said shut up!"

Alfred kept squeezing his bladder, and nothing kept coming out. He finally resorted to

139

thrusting his hips toward the pond before turning back to Hammercock.

"What is it already?" Alfred asked.

"Your…your peehole."

"What?" Alfred was still holding his penis in his hand. He lifted the head and looked down. "Sheeeeeeyut."

Where he should have had a urinary meatus was nothing but smooth, unbroken, rounded skin.

Chapter 19. Roll Through the Mess

There was blood all over the floor just outside the cafeteria. It looked like someone had tried mopping the floor with it, gave up, then came back and started again in another spot. Median was a little surprised the floor hadn't been cordoned off while someone cleaned it up, but then he reminded himself this wasn't a *real* hospital.

The blood was also the same color as a Red Rocket Pop. His mouth started watering, though in truth, he didn't want one. At least, not consciously.

He and Thomas T. Telford did their best not to roll through the mess, but it was impossible to completely avoid. There was a woman behind the front desk, chewing on an apple like it was an ear of corn, and he waved to her.

"Excuse me," Median said. "Is someone going to clean up all of this blood?"

She looked at him like he was the size of a fly, and Thomas T. Telford tapped him on the shoulder.

"Best not to ask them to look at anything around here too hard. She's human and alive, so she can't see what this place really looks like. Hell, you're alive and you don't see all of it. Imagine what *I* see."

Median gave the old man his best are-you-for-real expression, and Thomas T. Telford's eyes stayed on him.

"Half of 'im's still over there." He thumbed over to his right, and Median looked, but all he saw was more blood. "And there's a set of bones still in

141

a T-shirt and a pair of jeans inside the vestibule."
He shrugged.

Their hands got slicked with blood when
they rolled across the floor, and Median did his best
to ignore the sticky on his fingers and beneath his
nails and the coppery smell blending with
antiseptic. Never had he wanted to wash more—and
people had jizzled across his hands on many porn
shoots!

Thomas T. Telford hit the button for the
elevator, and the doors cranked open. Someone had
made a crude drawing of a demon's head. Its tongue
thrust into an "X" for a hole on a genderless person
with arms and legs akimbo, hanging upside down
and a surprised-sad look on their face.

"Is that new?" Median asked.

"Uh, yeah."

They turned their wheelchairs around, and
Median thumbed the button for their floor.

"I drew it," Thomas T. Telford said.

They got off the elevator, and Median
noticed the blood on their wheels and hands had
begun to flake off. He sniffed his hand and only
smelled the rubber but still made a mental note to
give them both a good scrub when he got back to
his room. Median needed to ask Thomas T. Telford
something but remained silent until they returned,
not wanting anyone to overhear.

"Why do you do it?" he asked once they
were both back in bed.

Thomas T. Telford had every ability to walk
the same as he did, but the wheelchair added to his
"old man mystique," as he put it.

"The window thing." The old man said it like it wasn't a question.

"Yeah."

"It's my loophole. Everyone's got one."

"I don't. I spent my whole life falling down every flight of stairs I could find."

"Then you, my friend, are exactly where you belong. I mean, you were already living hell. Why *not* come on over? I mean, I'm sorry about your circumstances, being alive and all and waiting on Beelzebuddy to chew you up on his wedding day, but let's be honest. One way or another, you were coming."

Median didn't take offense for some strange reason. Perhaps it was because a man who was absolutely certain of his own proper placement in hell telling him he was bound to come too was sort of a professional opinion. He wasn't entirely sure he understood, though.

"Say more," Median said.

"Huh? Oh, well, look at you, son. Good lookin' guy like you, you seem pretty smart. I know you're black and all, but damn if you didn't drop at least a dozen opportunities while you were up there."

"How would you know that?"

Thomas T. Telford made a face at him. "Tell me I'm wrong."

"No," Median said after a long moment.

He thought about his life. How he had let chances for something better slip through his fingers. Mary, most of all. He occasionally thought about what his life would have been like had he actually fought for her. Median was just so used to letting life happen to him, he never really considered doing something other than what he thought the world expected of him.

When he stirred from his own reverie, Thomas T. Telford was standing at the open window.

"You're going to do it again?" Median asked.

"You betcha. Hey, I meant to tell ya. *Canned*...you were *excellent* in that. Well, I got an early start for tomorrow. Take care, kid."

"See you around?"

And with that, the old man climbed over the sill and disappeared.

Tomorrow was the day. Median wasn't sure what he was going to do, but somehow...someway...he was going to fuck some shit up.

Chapter 20. How to Fuck Shit Up

The game plan had been to storm St. Eloise Hospital, find Dr. Rick, and throttle him until he let Walker go. He wasn't a big guy, and security had seemed virtually nonexistent. She could probably have the whole thing wrapped up in time for *The Bachelor*.

But Mary had fallen asleep. All that food…She'd barely made it upstairs before passing out in the hall.

Mary checked the time on her phone, which hardly had a charge, and saw she'd slept at least ten hours. Today was the last day. Despite feeling like a mountain with feet, Mary got up and went to the bathroom.

After she was done, she took a quick shower and brushed her teeth. Mary was thankful for her short hair. Derek had convinced her she'd be cute with a pixie cut when she'd been on the fence about it.

By the time she was out of the shower and dried off, the cramp going down her left side was finally starting to ease. Mary took the time to moisturize and put on eyeliner, some purple eyeshadow, and a little blush. She'd apply gloss in the car to save time.

Mary headed for the basement. Her step was a little lighter, and her face looked thinner in the mirror. It wasn't normal for a pregnant woman to lose weight, but nothing about this pregnancy was normal. Mary was due sometime today, when she hadn't been pregnant a week ago.

She kept her armory down here and figured a proper display of power was in order for what she was going to do. Mary had the intention to out-satan satan.

Her agreement with him had been to pick either her baby or her husband. She'd unquestioningly chosen her baby. But that didn't mean she couldn't *steal* Walker. No part of their agreement had stated she couldn't.

Of course, that didn't mean the devil couldn't just come and take him back. One step at a time, though. Her plan was a work in progress.

Mary wanted to hit them with overwhelming force, to cripple them before they knew they were in a fight. She reached for her Taurus 454, then had a thought. Mary was pregnant. Dr. Rick was her obstetrician. She might be able to walk right up to him if she played her cards right. Once they were alone in an examination room, a .25 Baby Browning might be enough to do the trick. Mary could tuck that away in her purse or put it in the waistband of her underwear.

She figured he might need some convincing beyond the threat of a handgun and decided to pack a few more items. Mary grabbed some bungee ties, zip ties, matches, and two lighters. Mary had to search around in her linen closet until she found the knitting needles her father had given her for Christmas some years back.

She hadn't knitted in quite some time, recalling for just a moment the sweater-making competitions she and Dad had had when she was a teen. Mary had stopped knitting for some reason she couldn't recall and made a note to revisit the hobby when this was all over. Her baby should have something homemade anyway.

The needles would have a much different purpose in the immediate future. The packaging stated the sizes went from "6.0 to 19.0 millimeters", and she nodded. The male urethra was eight to nine millimeters at the opening of the meatus, and she figured, more than likely, the threat of shoving anything up there would be enough to scare any man into compliance. But Dr. Rick wasn't *any* man. This might be a kink for him, and she might need to hurt him a little—or a lot—to break him. If she'd had a glass knitting needle, he definitely wouldn't enjoy her breaking *that* while it was inserted in his urethra.

Despite her lack of professional medical training, she'd catheterized men before. This definitely wasn't that, but Mary was certain she could do what needed to be done without permanent injury, if it came to that.

She paused and thought for a moment, wondering if it were possible to cripple the devil. And what if he weren't normal down there? What if it looked like ground beef or had an odd shape, like a pyramid or something? She resigned herself to the idea that as long as it had a hole she could shove stuff into, her idea would work.

While she'd been retrieving the things she needed, she'd come across several stashes of Derek's protein bars. *Stashes* probably wasn't the proper word. He was absentminded and tended to leave things all over the house, like a squirrel. He'd mail-ordered them from the Czech Republic, and at first, she'd just passed them by while she'd been searching. But on a lark, she turned one over. Surprisingly, the Czech word for "protein" was "protein". And one of these bars was chocked with fifty grams.

Mary collected all the ones she subsequently found and went back for the few she'd passed over. She hit the jackpot when she found an unopened box of them below the bottom shelf in her pantry.

She wasn't hungry but found herself gnawing on one while she hauled everything she was going to need to the garage. Mary had a key to Derek's Hummer and decided it was the better option, in case she needed to go off-road at any point. Plus, if his vehicle got destroyed instead of her loaner, it would serve him right.

She paused on the running board after opening the driver's side door. The scent of sandalwood wafted into her nose and whatever essence had come from Derek. Mary missed him. She didn't understand the anger she'd felt earlier and figured the two of them could sit down and talk when she got on the other end of this.

It never crossed her mind that the last time she'd seen this vehicle, it had been in the parking lot where her Lamaze class had been.

Mary started the engine and hit the button to open the garage door.

The radio came on. It was playing "Knockin' da Boots" by H-Town.

She turned it up.

a lowercase hell

Chapter 21. God's Little Eraser

Once Alfred had been able to stop screaming, he'd pieced it out logically. He was in heaven. Everything here was perfect. There was no need to produce waste because everything consumed was utilized. After some self-examination and independent verification, he was able to confirm he *did* have a butthole, but he realized he probably would never need to defecate in this place.

But he wanted a peehole, dammit!

Hammercock seemed to have accepted this change in his own anatomy without complaint. He was a simpleton, though, and that was in keeping with his personality. Urinating was meant to be an affront against a status quo, an everyman offense to show his dissatisfaction with his portion. Alfred felt he had been silenced and refused to accept his "voice" being taken away. Despite prizing himself as a man of the world, this was a deep insult to his sense of Americanism.

Upon further examination, he could feel he *did* have a urethra. In the spot where it should have been was a small depression. It was like his hole had been erased, a correction after the fact.

"You're not s'posed to play with it." Morgan stared at him so intently, Alfred turned around. The other man walked in front of him again. "It makes the trees and the ground sad-mad."

"What?" Alfred asked, still preoccupied with himself.

"The trees. And the ground. They get sad-mad when you play with it."

"Well, fuck the trees, and *fuck* the ground," Alfred said with as much venom as he could muster. He was the victim here. A key piece of his anatomy had been stolen.

"Oh." Morgan backed away.

Alfred shouldn't have been surprised when the ground opened under his feet and he fell in the crack, but he had still been preoccupied with himself and fell far enough to snap his shin. He rolled around in agony, the compound fracture one of the worst pains he'd ever felt in his life—death— *whatever!*

There was the sound of scree falling nearby, and a moment later, Hammercock was by his side. "Don't worry, angel," he said. "I know what to do."

Hammercock grabbed his ankle, and Alfred screamed, "Don't touch it!" He tried to swat the man away. Then Morgan was there too, holding him down by the shoulders.

"I'm going to help you like you helped me," Hammercock said.

For a moment, Alfred thought he saw the slightest hint of glee in the man's eyes. Alfred tried kicking him with his good leg, but Hammercock stepped back and to the side, pulling on his foot.

Alfred had been wrong. *This* pain was the worst he'd ever felt. Everything went a blinding white, razors scraping naked nerve endings. Alfred didn't recall blacking out, but suddenly, Morgan was there with a cup in his hand, pouring water over his mouth.

Alfred coughed and rolled away from him, spitting up water. Morgan kept trying to pour water in his mouth until Alfred knocked the cup out of his hands. He swatted blindly at the idiot.

"Stop! Stop!" Alfred shouted.

Morgan stood back and stared.

"Hammercock, where are you?" Alfred didn't know if Morgan was going to try to attack him again and thought he might need the man to help defend him.

He looked around. This wasn't just some hole in the ground. There were pillars, at least partially intact, and a marble floor. Why was this placed buried?

Alfred carefully stood and found he was able to put a good deal of his weight on his "broken" leg. He limped around what looked like a throne room until he came to the throne itself, split down the middle. It was *huge*. Whoever had sat on this throne must have been over nine meters tall. The answer as to who had sat here was obvious, and had he not been in heaven, Alfred would have denied *His* existence. He felt a little bit of a chill, though, at the thought of god not only existing, but seemingly unseated and…buried. Alfred wondered how such a thing could have happened.

He was able to grab onto the side of the ruby-studded silver throne and haul himself up. Morgan followed, and Alfred was secretly thankful. He limped across the seat and peered into the crack. Alfred was shook.

"H-Hammercock?" Alfred didn't like the sound of his voice and cleared the imaginary frog from his throat. "Hammercock, are you in there?"

Soft bluish-green light came from the crack, and when Alfred looked, there appeared to be a jagged tunnel. Alfred reached into the crack to pull himself up and was surprised at how sharp it was. He gripped it as carefully as he could and climbed inside, turning back to help Morgan. In truth, he didn't want to go in here on his own.

The tunnel led in a straight path they followed for a distance. Dim light emanated from the smooth walls. There was an opening ahead, and he half dreaded what he would see on the other side. Alfred lost his balance and reached out to steady himself on a wall. His hand came away wet with bluish-green goo. He had thought the tunnel was just lit by the stuff, but it was smeared with it.

Alfred could make out Hammercock's silhouette at the other end, just standing there, and he wondered why the man hadn't answered him.

"Hammercock! What are you doing?"

He didn't move. The whole situation made Alfred want to turn around and run, but he'd lived his entire life not being afraid of anything. He'd even returned from his own "death" after Milo had thought he'd killed him. Alfred had long prior lost the ability to die by any traditional means, and yet, here he was, so he had no doubt of his mortality. But what could possibly be death after death?

They finally reached the end of the tunnel, and it dropped off into an antechamber of sorts. The space was roughly carved and filled with all kinds of junk stuffed into the relatively small space. But what caught Alfred's eye was the same thing Hammercock must have been staring at for a prolonged period of time. If it was what it looked like, Alfred fully understood.

It was a large mass of something like muscle, and it obviously had come from something living. Well, living-adjacent. Alfred stumbled and reached for what he thought was only a column of some kind, but it was the only thing remaining in this space that could have been considered "alive". He steadied himself but looked at it as Knowledge surged into and through him, suffusing him with an amount of information equal to and beyond what he'd lost from drinking from the fountain.

Waves of memory flooded into his mind— of himself but not from his perspective. A ghost of a man holding him as a baby, adoring him, handing him to an older woman, and that woman feeding him. The memories fast forwarded, but he was still able to ingest them as they went—seeing himself as a two-year-old being brought into town by white men who worked on Cannonade Plantation. Alfred had remembered throwing a tantrum until they'd had no choice but to give in.

In the general store, a white boy no more than six pointed at him and Milo and laughed at their clothes and used a word—a word Alfred had heard but never understood. The men with him had surrounded the boy and the person Alfred presumed was his father. Alfred remembered this, but he'd never seen what had happened to the two of them after. A couple of the men with him had roughly

shoved the boy and his father out of the general
store and beaten the both of them, breaking the
man's arm for good measure before leaving them
there and returning inside. The man who had stayed
with Alfred had bought him some chocolates and
consoled him as if Alfred had been the one who'd
been broken.

The word had stuck with him, though, and
over the next few months, as his every indulgence
had been granted, Alfred became monstrous,
demanding more and more of the men and women
who worked and lived on Cannonade. Alfred had
taken joy at ripping Ma'am Davies's tit from her
bodice and feeding in front of everyone. He smiled
now, although his face felt like it was a billion light
years away from the rest of his body. Alfred, the
child, continued his reign of terror until one of the
men—Will, his name had been—called him that
word, and in that moment, it had clicked there was a
wide-running river of difference between people
who had skin like his and people who had skin like
Will's.

And he hated him for that. He hated *all* of
them for that.

The hatred he'd felt inside him had boiled
out. It had become a life unto itself and had touched
the man. The man had shaken and jittered, foaming
at the mouth until it moved away from him to find
someone else. The man's eyes had gone glassy
black, and he'd walked over to the stairs, yanked at
one of the spindles of the banister until it came free,
and then opened his mouth and shoved it through
his head.

155

The formless thing had gone on touching people throughout the great house, including his momma, whom he hated too. With each person, it diminished, but its effect remained constant. Everyone either immediately killed themselves, began setting fire to the house, or found someone outside and killed them.

Until Milo and Isis.

They hadn't known Union soldiers were advancing on the plantation. It was thoroughly burning by the time the three of them had fled. Alfred hadn't recalled seeing the thing that had come out of him; he'd simply remembered being angry. But was there more to it? Had he felt something almost like a guiding hand of sorts, pushing and pulling at him?

Yes, the memories from whatever the entity was had given him a perspective he'd never been able to consider before. Alfred had wanted all those horrible things to happen. But by the same token, he hadn't been the *only* one wanting them. There was another with him, leading him to do the awful things he'd been doing. It became even clearer when the memories of him grew older and he saw more people he'd hurt.

Andy Mayfield had been the first boy he'd kissed, and thirteen-year-old Alfred didn't know what to do with the feelings coursing through him. Milo tried to tell him not to, that carrying on with a boy was bad enough. But his being white added to it could be dangerous to the both of them. Alfred remembered telling Milo he didn't care and that he would live his life on his terms, but he could now see that force guiding him to do such *horrible* things to little Andy.

And then Christie Menton when he was seventeen…And Barbara and Jules on his twenty-first birthday…He'd always thought it had been him doing it. That he'd been at the helm of his own mind. But there had been something with him, encouraging him if not outright controlling him.

Alfred felt the tears in his eyes when he realized he'd been a tool all his life. The memories raced by, and it only became more apparent. While he thought he'd been the master of his domain, he'd simply been the instrument of some hidden being until he'd been stopped by *her*.

By Mary…

For the first time, he felt gratitude for the woman who had murdered him. He could see himself through his own eyes and through the book—the tree. Alfred looked at it. A trunk as thick as his thigh, growing out of the floor of the antechamber to chest height, where its branches spread open. It looked like a pulpit, its leaves large and square, the venation-like skrit the likes he'd never seen before.

They were words, he knew, but they weren't read with the eyes. They were read with the soul. And as they had uploaded the story of his life into him, they'd also written a great deal more information beneath. He could feel the hum inside him, the sheer amount of data written into the cells of his body, and though he wasn't conscious of all of it at once, he knew it was there and knew he could access it anytime he wanted.

The thing Hammercock and Morgan both stared at—the thing the size of a compact car—had left a trail of blood and was even now oozing traces of ichor from the giant gash nearly bisecting it.

A heart.

"I think they murdered god," Alfred said.

Chapter 22. Meal with the Devil

She came to him just as he expected.
Median felt like he was awake, but considering how
he had woken up after the two prior nights when
she'd visited him, he guessed he had to be
dreaming.

She had on that same too-short nurse's
outfit, with the cap like before, and when she stood
in the lit doorway, she took the time to pull on a
dishwashing glove before coming over and
grabbing Median firmly by the crotch.

"Evening, lover," she said in Dr. Rick's
voice.

"Hey, can we, um…talk first?"

She regarded him with those red coal eyes a
moment, then stood upright. "What do you want to
know? How you're gonna die tomorrow? Do you
want to *beg* me for mercy?"

"No. I just…wanna understand. Why me?"

She coughed a laugh. "If I had a Lydian for
every time somebody asked me that." She shook her
head. "I'll do you one better. How do you like your
roommate?"

"Thomas T. Telford? He's okay. Why?"

"Oh, is that his name?" She laughed again.
"Imagine thinking you can find a loophole out of
your punishment in hell by jumping out a window.
How much do you think it hurts when you hit the
ground? Do you think there's a flash and then it's
over? Maybe you linger in agony for a couple
hundred milliseconds?"

"I don't understand. You know?"

159

She laughed a full, throaty Dr. Rick laugh. "Just because half the staff are idiots doesn't mean I'm the one fooled. Like you've been."

"What do you mean?"

"Here. Have one." She presented him a Red Rocket Pop out of nowhere, and he took it.

Median unwrapped it and was about to start eating it before he realized he didn't actually want it. He dropped it on the floor. It might have felt real, but it wasn't. This was only a dream.

The nurse regarded the Rocket Pop on the floor with an expression of sadness. "Thomas T. Telford was a horrible man," she said, still looking down. "He deserves everything he gets in hell. It's a shame he got to die peacefully in his sleep."

Median shook his head. "He didn't die in his sleep. He said his ex-wives killed him."

She cocked her head to one side.

"Oh my god. He isn't Thomas T. Telford?"

She pointed her finger like a gun and shot.

"Then who?"

"Nigel Vorhees-Ingwerson lived a very monkish life. Never married, no kids—by choice—donated half his accountant's salary to charity, donated blood regularly, donated a *kidney*, tutored at the library, volunteered at the museum, *blah, blah, blah*. Tell me something. What happens when you live a good life and then you die?"

"You...go to heaven?"

"And what happens when you live a bad life and then you die?"

"Hell." Median nodded like a schoolboy.

"How about if you live an arguably good
and charitable life but you feel like you haven't
done enough? That your shortcomings are so great
that you are no better than someone who murders or
litters?" She sat on the edge of his bed and placed
her hands in her lap, the gloved one atop the other.

"You—"

"Come *here*. Exactly!" She quietly clapped
her hands together. "Where you work out a story in
your head that you were the worst person in the
world and when you died you were so awful, you
figured out a loophole so you could even get over
on the *devil*."

"Oh my god. For real?"

The nurse stood and walked over to the
other bed. She stripped off the blanket and lay face
down on the bed sheet. Her skirt was high enough
Median got a good view. She wasn't wearing
panties and was *very* pierced.

"Mmm, I loooooove cool bed sheets!"

"I think I understand," Median said. "All my
life, I've been hard on myself. I haven't been able to
experience the good in my life. To just…enjoy it. I
was married to a beautiful woman. We couldn't
have had kids, but we could've adopted. I mean, we
had a whole life ahead—"

"*Wrong*!" The devil-woman leapt on
Median's bed. She began jumping up and down and
shouting, a maniacal smile on her face. "Wrong!
Wrong! Wrong! Wrong! Wrong! Wrong!" She sat
on the opposite end of his bed with her legs folded.
"You thought this place was a reprieve from hell.
It's not. It's just a more creative way of torturing

the damned." She held up her gloved hand and wiggled her fingers. "Now, what do you say to a nice prostate milking?"

Median shook his head. "I don't want that."

"Come on already, Walker. I don't have all night. I have to give an enema at two to somebody who's really queasy about butt stuff. I could use the practice."

"You're a liar. You're lying to me."

"No-no. I can't tell you who because of HIPAA, but I really do."

"I don't mean that. I mean about Thomas T. Telford. Or Nigel Swervson."

"Vorhees-Ingwerson."

"Whatever. That name sounds made-up. You probably saw it on a kiddy playpark or Ikea."

She shrugged.

That shrug turned wheels in Median's mind. "Wait a minute. Why am *I* here? Really? Why am I so important that you wanted me alive? There has to be a million people you could have yanked down here to eat for your…for your wedding. Is it even me? Am I the one you really want?"

The devil woman smiled wide, showing off several rows of triangular shark teeth. Her hands caught his eye. Her fingers were elongating. "So…should we get started?"

"No," he said. "No!" Median drew back both feet and kicked her in the chest, pitching her over the bed.

A normal human would have at least been stunned or even injured, but he wasn't counting on

a lowercase hell

her staying down. Median was already hard and
went to work on himself under the covers.

"Oh, yeah," the devil woman said in Dr.
Rick's voice. "Now you're gettin' me hot."

Median beat off furiously while her nurse
cap slowly rose into view. He'd masturbated dry
often enough but never this intensely and could feel
himself chafing. At the same time, though, there
was something kind of hot about being in danger, if
not the outright risk of death. He began to climax,
when those coal-red eyes appeared.

"What do you think you're doing?" she said
in her feminine voice, her eyes going wide. "You
stop. Stop right now, or I'll gouge your eyes out!"
She wriggled over the edge of the bed like a worm,
boneless and slow, just as Median felt the first pulse
of his orgasm.

Median's breathing was fast and ragged. His
hips pumped while she hovered above the bed,
readying to strike, her fingers twisting and
elongating into bony knives and—

"Mr. Harris. Mr. Harris! Sir!"

Median screamed when he opened his eyes.
A doctor he'd never seen before was extra close,
flashing a penlight onto his face. He was still
breathing fast and felt congealing sweat crawling
down his skin.

"Okay, he's awake," the doctor said, putting
the penlight back in her lab coat's breast pocket.
She flashed her eyes down at his arm and then back
to his eyes. "Um, Mr. Harris, could you stop,
um…doing that?"

"Huh?" Median felt like he was still catching up to speed. He glanced at his arm and saw it was shaking—no...*jerking*...

"Oh. Um. Of course." He put his hands to either side of his hips, aware of the tent in the middle of his blanket. Median felt...dry...The orgasm must have just been in his nightmare.

Two male nurses came in, and the doctor stepped back.

"I'm Dr. Healy," she said, tucking an errant lock of raven hair behind her ear. "These gentlemen are going to take you for prep before your procedure."

"Procedure?" Median asked. "What procedure? I'm only here for my arm, and you guys did that the night I got here."

"Could you state your full name and D-O-B?" she asked.

The nurses stood to either side of the bed, and one of them began pressing latches and switches and whatever else beneath it. The other unplugged him from the machines monitoring his life signs.

"Walker Median Harris," he said, then gave his date of birth. He tried keeping eye contact with the doctor while she backed out of the room and they began wheeling him out.

"We'll just need you to sign these three release forms." Dr. Healy held the clipboard out to him, and he reached but pulled his hand back.

"I'm not signing that."

His looping signature had already been scrawled next to the sloppily written "X"s at the bottom of all three pages.

"Oh, you're declining anesthesia?" she asked, surprised.

"No! That's not my signature. I didn't sign that."

"So you *do* want anesthesia? This can be a very invasive procedure. It's going to take hours to put everything back where it's supposed to be."

"Yes. No. I don't know. I don't want any surgery. What's happening? Where are you taking me?"

Dr. Healy fell behind while the two burly nurses continued pushing his bed down the hall. Median looked around, desperately trying to figure out where he was going and wishing he could say something, just to make them stop. They wheeled him onto an elevator, where the only other person was a timid-looking thin man holding a few sheets of paper.

"Help me," Median whispered, knowing full well the two nurses could hear him.

The timid-looking man glanced at him nervously, then straight ahead, adjusting his tie.

"Well, this is my stop," the man said, pulling a button on the panel.

A bell rang, and the doors opened between floors. The man tried to scurry to the upper one by using the edge of Median's bed to leverage himself. But he was still not able to get through.

"A little help?" he asked.

One of the massive nurses turned, grabbed both ankles in one hand, and lifted, shoving the man by the ass with the other.

The nurse pushed the button back, silencing the bell, and the doors slid shut. The car continued, and he returned to Median's side.

Median inspected the two men for the first time. They were the biggest human beings he'd ever seen in person. They didn't look alike, but they had the same expression—post-post-traumatic stress disorder with wide open, lidless, coal-black eyes and mouths downturned in permanent grimaces. One had tattoos on his neck that looked like dozens of tails trailing to some kind of monster beneath his shirt. Their heads were buzzed and lumped with muscle or old scar tissue. The tattoo-less one had a dash of white skin through his eyebrow and a deep carve in a C-shape across one cheek.

They wheeled him into a room which looked like it had been abandoned. Ceiling tiles were either missing or stained a varying shade of brown. A door shut, and a bright lamp clicked on. They wheeled him to the foot of a table and grabbed him roughly under his arms and thighs, lifting him and dropping him onto the metal.

Median felt like a baby beneath the mercy of the two brutes. He uselessly tried fighting them off while they put his wrists and ankles in manacles. Then they put another restraint around his chest and hips. Medium finally got the idea to scream for help, as useless as that would be, and the one with the tattoos on his neck shoved a bit in Median's mouth.

A man in a plaid shirt and circular block glasses hovered into view. He held big cards to his chest and flicked one in front of Median. The first was what looked like the silhouette of a bird with a plus sign and a tree. Then he switched it for an amorphous blob, like the outline of an eldritch god, a plus sign, and a blank line.

"Anything?" the man asked.

"What?" Median said.

"Perfect." He turned left.

"What? What *perfect*? Perfect-good? Perfect-bad?"

Median tried to spit it out, but it was really jammed in there to the point the joints of his jaw ached. The corners of his lips felt like they were on the verge of tearing. The other nurse hovered over him, then used his sausage fingers to pry open Median's eyelids, putting in drops that felt like bees pricking him in the eyes. One of them might have jammed a needle into his hip, but Median was temporarily blinded and couldn't see what they were doing.

By the time his vision had returned to blurry, the table he was strapped to was buzzing. This had to be it. Today was the day Dr. Rick was getting married, so this had to be the prep before they ate him. Maybe this was some sort of marinade, or that shot was some sort of juice he was going to baste in. Any moment now, one of these brutes would probably start chopping him into steaks.

The foot of the table lifted, and his legs were roughly spread apart by whatever machinery controlled it. Median was spun over, facing the floor, until he had a view of the mechanical guts directing the arm the table was connected to. The smell of oil and heat filled his nose, and the table made incremental movements, centering him for something. Blood rushed to his head, making the dancing crimson and blue spots in his vision pulse even bigger. The table rotated again, and he was looking at the orange sodium lamps overhead. Air blew up his gown, then his chest and face. Median's vision cleared just in time to see the red target appear on his torso, slowly anchoring down to his crotch.

There were several semi-distant beeps while he looked around, panicked and hoping to make one final plea to the two nurses. Other than the atonal humming of several machines, he was all alone.

Two more machines descended from the ceiling on robotic arms—one shaped like an overhead projector, the other like a compact knurling machine. Its ridged wheels spun in one direction, then quickly reversed.

They got really close to his junk. Really, *really* close.

"Please, god, no!" Median yelled. He'd always thought he'd be able to withstand torture. That if he were compromised and in the hands of the enemy—whoever that might have been—he would be able to withstand whatever they did to him. Median had broken bones before and never thought the pain—though great—would have been enough to make him yield any secrets entrusted to him.

But now, it was apparent pain wasn't strictly necessary to break him. He whimpered. The two machines aimed at his genitalia made at least thirty seconds of mechanical noises, narrowing tolerances, alternating with clicks, remeasuring hums, and whirs, conversing in their own mechanical language. He pulled as hard as he could against his restraints.

A sound escaped him, more animal than the rational, intelligent being he always had thought of himself as. Then the knurling machine shook, and they both rotated back into the ceiling.

A thing a lot like the down-telescope on a submarine lowered and was within a hair's breadth of the red target on his crotch. Median willed everything down there to just crawl up inside him, not wanting whatever was about to happen to happen. The down-telescope thing spun left, then right, emitting a high-pitched *Eeeeeee* each time it moved.

Median had always thought of himself as mentally tough, a solid wall. He had to be to perform on camera. But now he felt his sanity slowly lift off him like a blanket in the night, hovering almost out of his reach.

The familiar *click-whirrr* of an old Polaroid camera...

Median looked around, and the telescope thing lifted back into the ceiling. Someone stood in front of the door.

Dr. Rick.

He was waving the self-developing picture with a big smile, the camera in his other hand. "You should see the look on your face right now," he said, laughing. "Aw, man. Priceless."

"What? What?" Median said, tears still streaming from his eyes, glazed sweat cooling all over his body.

"How do I explain?" Dr. Rick rolled his eyes to the ceiling. "This is like my own little version of *Punk'd.* None of this stuff is really used for anything." He opened the panel of one of the machines. Dozens of multi-colored lights blinked inside. "'Least I don't think so." He tried to shut it, but the panel snapped off in his hand. Dr. Rick laid it gently on a counter.

He started undoing the straps, and some sort of liquid shot Median in the face. Median squealed, and that made Dr. Rick laugh even harder. He was more than a little shaky when he got off the table, suddenly cold, and huddled around himself.

Dr. Rick put an arm around his shoulders, and they began to walk toward the door. "Look, I'd be lying if I said I'm not nervous about today. Y'know, getting married and all. I guess this was my way of letting off a little pressure."

Median was so shaken, he leaned on him for support. "Okay," he said, not able to cobble together a coherent thought yet.

For the first time, Dr. Rick was in a tuxedo.

"You know, I'm really glad you're here. It might be hard to believe, but I don't have a lot of friends. I mean, maybe you and I aren't exactly friends, but we have history, y'know?"

"Uh-huh?"

"I know that's a long ways from actual friendship, but there's not a long track record of people who have 'history'"—Dr. Rick made wiggly quotation marks with the index and middle fingers of his free hand—"with me either. I just really wanted to have somebody down here who hadn't been damned, cursed, banished, denounced, castigated, removed, doomed, convicted, censured, or had blasphemed. Believe it or not, that doesn't leave a lot of folks."

"So…you don't want to eat me?" Median asked. They walked a dark, narrow hallway.

"What?" Dr. Rick looked shocked. "Why would you think that?"

"That's what they told me."

"Who is 'they'?"

Median thought a moment and realized he couldn't recall. Dr. Rick waved him off.

"Never mind. That's not important. I *get* why someone might've thought that, but let me tell you, they got it wrong. Let's chalk it up to…mistranslation. I *do* need you in the ceremony, but I need *you* to eat something, not the other way around."

"Me *eat*?" Blood was still gradually returning to Median's brain.

"Yeah!" Dr. Rick laughed again and gave him a shake. "And it's not something gross or anything, like rotten flesh or the egg of some lesser beast."

He looked at Median with a wide grin, like he was expecting to be asked what. When Median didn't say anything for a long moment, Dr. Rick's smile dropped.

"Okay, not to come off like the guy constantly looking to poke a finger in You-Know-Who's eye, but let me ask you something…Why did Adam and Eve eat?"

Median shook his head. "I don't know."

"Exactly! I mean, back when they were in the Garden of Eden, there was no such thing as illness. No such thing as death. And don't give me that 'Well, the g-man *designed* their bodies to eat.' The human body is also designed to be able to run, but when was the last time your Uncle Jeff even looked at a treadmill?"

"Uncle Jeff" wasn't actually Median's uncle, but a former neighbor his parents had kept in contact with after he'd moved. The man had been two hundred fifty pounds when Median was five and three hundred fifty pounds when he was fifteen. He'd been one of the nicest people Median had ever known—although now, Median suspected his parents might have involved him in some threesome situations—and was long practiced in being as still as possible in any given situation. Uncle Jeff had had arthritis in his knees and gout in his ankles.

"Think about what motivated Adam to take that first bite of…whatever it was. What made him think, 'Hey, I'm gonna grab the thing that fell off that tree or pull up some of that stuff from the ground and put it in my mouth.' Even before he actually did it, there had to be a genetic imperative, something that told him to 'eat'—whatever that meant. He wasn't given any instructions. He couldn't have appreciated the dynamics of using his incisors to bite off a piece of something and then use his molars to masticate it to the point where it was swallowable. Exactly *what* could have instructed him to do such a thing? And you can't rely on genetic history because there simply *was* no such thing."

Median just stared at him.

"It was desire. Good ol' *lust*. That thing that told him to do it for no other reason than because he could. And when you think about it, if he'd choked…do you think god would have given him the Heimlich? I mean, just consider for a second…Ask yourself, would He have made any discernible distinction between choking and swallowing? One would have been interminable discomfort, the other sating some innate desire he had no intention of ever informing Adam he had."

"But god told him there was food," Median said.

Dr. Rick shook his head. "He told him there was food. But he never explained what food was or what to do with it. 'Lo, I have given to you every herb sowing seed, which is upon the face of all the earth, and every tree in which is the fruit of a tree sowing seed, to you it is for food.' Now tell me, where in there is instruction on what to do with food or even how to identify what *wasn't* food?"

"The seeds," Median said.

"Ever eaten a potato? Where are potato seeds? What do *they* look like? And again, where is the instruction on how to identify what a seed is?"

Dr. Rick shook his head. "I'm getting all worked up over old business. That's not what you're here for!"

They'd been walking in a dark hallway, but suddenly, Median was semi-blinded by light. He held up his hands, blinking until his vision was adjusted, and saw he was in a dressing room. There were at least a dozen people in here in various outfits, dressed like they were going someplace special, like a wedding.

Dr. Rick grabbed a fistful of Median's gown and ripped it off. Median covered himself, expecting to be exposed to everyone there. Despite his part-time work in the adult film industry, he was shy about getting naked in non-sexual situations.

Instead of being nude, though, Median had on his own black tuxedo, complete with blood-red carnation. He looked down at what should have been his bare feet and was surprised to see he had on a pair of shiny crimson and black Corthays. Median had never heard of such a shoe before and yet knew the name anyway.

"The first thing Adam ate was more than likely a fruit called a stardew. Pretty bitter, hard to find in its original form. I want *you* to eat it. It's a ceremonial first thing, kind of an affront to the big man. You aren't on the menu, man."

"For real?"

"Yeah. I mean, we gotta kill you for you to stay in hell, but I'm a *vegan*." Dr. Rick turned to a random woman in the room, pointed to Median, and said, "Hey, get this man a Red Rocket Pop, huh?" And back to Median. "Try not to get any on the tux. It's a rental, okay?"

For some reason, Median felt relieved. Someone—not who the devil had asked—handed him a Red Rocket Pop. He took it gratefully, his still unsteady hands having a hard time unwrapping it. Perhaps the idea of being eaten was probably one of the most terrifying ways to go. At least his death wasn't going to be a part of the wedding ceremony. So he still had time for his Hail Mary pass.

An organ somewhere in the distance began playing, and despite not ever hearing whatever the tune was in any church he'd ever been in, Median recognized the song. In fact, he was pretty certain he'd heard it on an organ before.

It was "Inna Gadda Da Vida."

"That's our sign, folks," a chubby demon in a poorly fitted off-the-rack black suit said, poking his head in the door.

The mostly men and women began filing hurriedly out of the room until only Dr. Rick and Median remained. The demon popped back in and pointed at Median with what he guessed were his index and middle fingers.

"You. Let's go, buddy. Gotta get you into posish." The demon looked at Dr. Rick. "Congrats, sir. Get up there and pull one for Dick!"

Median wasn't sure what getting "into posish" entailed. The demon knocked the popsicle out of his hands, but Median didn't like the sound of it. He'd hoped he would be able to hold the ring or be one of the guys who stood for the groom, or something. "Into posish" sounded a lot more…restrainy than he wanted.

"I'll see you up there." Dr. Rick slapped him on the back, and Median jumped.

He jumped again when he saw Dr. Rick's eyes. They were deep yellow, with dagger-like pupils. Median didn't know how to take the nervous smile on Dr. Rick's face, but the look was somewhat familiar. Dr. Rick had looked like that when he'd lied to Median about having to hurt him to strip the fetus out of him.

Median didn't know exactly how, but in some way, Dr. Rick was lying to him.

Chapter 23. Surprise Bullet

Once again, the parking lot was empty. Mary had been sitting in the Hummer for several minutes, trying to settle her breathing. She was nervous, and added to that, she was having contractions again. It couldn't be time yet. It just couldn't.

The feeling coursing through her was a distant cousin to the certainty she was going to vomit after having too much to drink. The weird thing was, she was hungry at the same time. She dabbed the sweat off her brow. The air conditioning was cranked all the way up, and all the vents pointed in her direction. After she'd eaten her third protein bar and chased it with half of a liter bottle of water, she began to feel normal—or at least, not like she was about to explode in a ball of flame.

If Mary was going to pull this off, she'd have to remain focused. She needed to talk her way into Dr. Rick's office and establish control. Mary had seen him injured, and that hopefully meant he was mortal. Maybe a gunshot wouldn't kill him, but it should sufficiently wound him to make him pliant for what would come after.

She killed the engine and slid out of the Hummer. Mary found herself feeling gradually better, approaching the building, and the heat inside her was reduced to a simmering flame by the time she was in the vestibule.

Mary refused to believe something was wrong with the baby. It was going to be Walker's, and that was bad enough. It just seemed like the more she tried to get away from him, the more she got tangled up in Walker's life.

In the lobby of St. Eloise, everything looked…different. For starters, the dead body, like it had been there for years, was new. The paint was peeling off the walls, the drop ceiling's tiles—what few there were—looked urine-stained, and the floor was mostly stripped down to the wood planking. But the front desk—and Maddy, ever so cheerful Maddy—was in pristine condition.

"Mrs. Harris!" she said with a smile in her voice. "Are you ready to check in?"

"Excuse me?"

"Dr. Rick is waiting for you. You're due today?"

That did more to chill Mary than the Hummer's air conditioning. The elevator doors cranked open from around the corner, and Mary waddled over in that direction with the sinking sensation what she'd planned wasn't going to work.

Mrs. Manhorn, standing in the elevator, waiting for her, wasn't a vote of confidence either.

"Good afternoon, Mrs. Harris," the old woman said. She had furrowed lines in her forehead, and her hairline looked too low.

Mary knew, if she looked at the back of the woman's head, there would be a deep gash in her scalp. Mrs. Manhorn looked a lot grayer than the last time Mary had seen her. Her face seemed to be more of a mask, and the lizard part of Mary's brain whispered that someone had peeled off Mrs. Manhorn's scalp and removed the cap of her skull to get a gander at the old woman's cerebellum.

"Mrs. Manhorn, are you okay?"

"No," the nurse said curtly. "I'm dead. But I am your doula, so I am here for you. As promised. I wouldn't miss it for my eternal soul."

Mary got on the elevator, noting the blackish brown stains across the front of the woman's outfit. Once the doors closed, the scent of sterility and death wafting off Mrs. Manhorn pushed Mary against the rear wall of the car.

It felt like the elevator was being pulled up by rope, hand over hand, jerking upward several feet, stopping, seeming to drop a foot or two—god, she hoped not—then dragging up again.

"I'm sorry about…what happened to you," Mary said.

"You mean when you *killed* me?" Mrs. Manhorn said without turning around. "Not to worry. You are a mother-to-be. You are prone to all sorts of understandable fits of emotion during this time."

She sure is taking her murder pretty well, Mary thought, squeezing the grab-bar behind her. She had a pretty good idea a gun wouldn't do too much to a dead woman who'd apparently rushed right over after her autopsy.

Despite her fear, Mary couldn't help but study the back of the woman's head where it had apparently been shaved, revealing the dent in her skull and the fold of exposed meat just under her scalp...The diagonal gash where her head had split open when she'd fallen...Her jet-black hair had been tugged and teased carelessly over the wound, obscuring it from anyone not staring directly at it.

Mary would have horror movie bingo if a beetle crawled out of that hole right now.

"I should probably say something to dissuade you," Mrs. Manhorn said.

"Excuse me?"

The woman didn't repeat herself. The elevator finally dinged, and the doors slid open smoothly when the car shivered to a stop.

"Watch your step," Mrs. Manhorn said, and Mary stepped out. "We'll see you upstairs. When you're done with the doctor."

Mary wanted to ask who all "we" was and why the woman—despite Mary having an idea Mrs. Manhorn suspected what she was up to—had just left her here alone. She didn't dare look at Mrs. Manhorn as she passed or turn around when the doors closed.

Mary hadn't been on this floor before and wasn't sure where to go. Until she saw the mostly dried corpse propped up on a bench, wearing a dress similar to something Mary had in her own closet…She mentally added a little bit of color and stuffing to the sallow cheeks, sat the body upright in her mind's eye, and was reasonably certain the corpse looked like her.

The corpse had a sign in its lap, propped up with a hand attached to the wrist by the thinnest thread of white tendon. It read, "Dr. Smith 126," in the same color brown as the gore beneath the bench, which had apparently dripped off the seated corpse.

Mary began checking the doorways and following them in ascending order. *108, 111, 117*…She passed by a couple of more corpses eerily like her, except one barely more than bones, wearing fatigues with a pair of hoop earrings somehow suspended from either side of its head, which Mary last remembered seeing at least five years ago. Another was in the jeans and white T-shirt she'd been wearing the night she'd been on the run with Median from the devil. That corpse was…fresh—obviously dead from its corkscrewed neck and head turned somewhere between one and two o'clock.

She found Room 126 and could make out someone inside through the glass window in the upper half of the door. It had to be Dr. Rick. Rather than hesitating, as her morbid dread was instructing her to do, Mary pushed into the room and saw the devil in question, writing something on a sheet of paper on a clipboard.

"Just a sec," Dr. Rick said, finishing writing. He scrawled something that could have been a signature at the bottom of the page and, walking Mary backward two steps, put the clipboard on a hook just outside the door.

"Hey, Mary. Come on in," he said.

Mary walked back in and closed the door behind her. She cleared her throat, even though she didn't know how to begin. Dr. Rick sat on his balance ball chair and wheeled back underneath his desk.

"How may I help you, Mrs. Harris?"

It was an odd question. She had no reason to be here, other than her baby. Mary took a long moment to respond.

"It's my baby," she said, shifting on her feet. "I want to keep her."

Dr. Rick shrugged. "So keep her. She's perfectly healthy. We can go upstairs right now and pop that thang right out of you, and you can start living happily ever after."

"I'm on board with all that. You know I've been wanting this baby pretty much my whole life. But the thing is—"

"You're having doubts about betraying your husband. You feel guilt."

He put his hand over hers on top of his desk. A second before, Mary had had both hands on her purse.

"Let me tell you something about guilt, Mrs. Harris. It's a reflex. Every human being wants something. Guilt is just a way of looking over your shoulder to see who's watching you have what you already decided to take. It's one of the nasty side-effects of evolution. Do you think an antelope feels sympathy for the mama lion and her cubs when they go hungry? The *world* is trying to eat you. Don't feel bad because you aren't in its mouth yet."

He pointed to her belly.

"Other than you, me, and Walker Harris, nobody knows about this deal. I didn't get to where I am by blabbing about all the moves I make. And your husband is—and will remain—in hell. Considering all of what people do to get into our non-exclusive club, do you really have anything to feel *guilty* about for the little bit you did?"

"I guess…I guess, no." For a brief moment, Mary felt a tickle of doubt. "At the same time, though," she said, "Walker didn't do anything to deserve going to hell."

"Sure, he did. He's a whoremaster. Do you know how many people he had sex with whom he was *not* married to? The bible is pretty straightforward about that. And you're his *wife*. He sinned against you, just as much as god."

"Yeah…I know…Still…I mean, human beings are a constant work in progress. Who knows where Walker would have wound up on his own? Our situation isn't as straightforward as that. And it's not like I haven't been with anybody since we separated."

Mary couldn't believe she was actually arguing against herself. For a moment, she couldn't remember exactly what she was arguing *for*. She found herself wondering where she was in Dr. Rick's twisted logic.

"His last…scene might have been his last, for all we know, and he could have become a preacher or something."

Dr. Rick nodded thoughtfully. "You know, you're right. He could have been on the verge of becoming the next Mother Theresa. *Daddy Terry*. But all we have to go on are his actual acts. Mary, your husband has been a whoremaster, taking payment for sex for the sake of depraved human beings in desperate need to pour into that unfillable void inside themselves. When you brought him to me, he wasn't anywhere close to making the world a better place. He's been assessed where he was because that's the only metric that truly matters. Neither one of us stopped him from doing whatever

183

he wanted to do with his life. Now had he been reciting the Lord's Prayer as he was being wheeled in here or something like that, I could see the argument, but…"

Walker had never been religious. Not that Mary had, but he was probably one of a handful of people she knew who just flat-out didn't care whether or not there was a god and whatever his plan might have been for mankind.

"You want to know if there is a path that exists for you to both keep your baby and for your husband to be set free from hell?" Dr. Rick lifted his hand from hers.

She put her hand back on her purse. He steepled his fingers and rested his elbows on his desk.

"No."

Her heart sank a little, but it wasn't an unexpected answer.

"Mary," Dr. Rick said, smiling. "Don't you know? It's you I want. All this time…it's been *you*."

"Me?" The skin on the back of her neck prickled.

"No. No." He waved her off. "It's a little late in the story to make a switch-up like that. Nobody would buy that. You're here to propose another deal. New terms and a change of stakes. It's not gonna happen, but let's hear it anyway."

"He's not my hus—" Mary took a deep breath to calm herself. She forced a smile, her way of resetting, and stood, calmly unzipping her purse, reaching in, and drawing the .25 Baby Browning before gutshooting him. "I'm not here for deals. This is a robbery."

He fell out of his chair and rolled around on the floor, moaning in agony while he bled.

"What the fuck?" he said—*asked*—sounding more surprised than in pain. "You shot me? I thought we were connecting!"

Mary wondered briefly if his response was typical for people who'd been caught by a surprise bullet. She didn't respond immediately, taking a good ten seconds to gather her thoughts before proceeding.

"You're going to set Walker free."

"The hell I am." Dr. Rick clutched his gut, dark crimson leaking between his fingers. "If I set him free, then your baby goes bye-bye." He slowly curled around his wound.

Mary shook her head. "Oh, no. Our deal is still in place. I picked my baby over my...husband." Calling Walker that made her shiver with discomfort. "Officially, my choice is my baby. I'm *stealing* him from you."

"What?" Dr. Rick looked in her general direction, his thin lips turning blue, in so much obvious pain his eyes hovered somewhere over her head, like he couldn't focus on her.

"You heard. I'm honoring our deal, *and* I'm stealing him."

"But you can't...But you can't do that."

"Of course, I can't," Mary said. "That's why I'm doing it. There's nothing in the contract that says it'll be voided if I steal him. If you don't release Walker Median Harris now, I'm going to do so many worse things than shooting you in the gut."

"You can't do this. I'm a respected member of the community. If you kill me, it's only a matter of time before the police knock on your door."

"Keep up the facade if it makes you feel better," Mary said. "I've got things in my purse that'll hurt you a lot more than a bullet."

"Okay." Dr. Rick stopped cradling himself and slowly straightened out.

Mary saw the clarity in his eyes and recognized he was about to get up. She pulled a C-shaped device on a necklace out of her purse and laid it over his neck. Dr. Rick's eyes went wide, and he inhaled a sharp breath.

"You assumed I came in here not knowing anything about you," she said. "I was in counterintelligence. I know how to research my enemy. You want to guess what else I have in here?" She waggled her little purse and gave Dr. Rick a half-smile.

"This is bullshit," Dr. Rick said, panting, his forehead coursing with sweat. "I gave you what you want. This isn't—"

"Fair?" Mary said, interrupting. "Tell me about your long and storied history of being fair with the people who make deals with you."

Dr. Rick grinned weakly. "All right. You got me on that one. But you have to know, I won't take you stealing from me lying down."

"Said the devil as he lay on the floor," Mary replied. "Let's take it one step at a time." She smiled at him. "You don't know that I don't already have a plan in place to make it not worth the effort to come after him."

"I'm gonna come after *you*."

"And that will be the worst possible mistake you could make. Do you like your necklace?"

Dr. Rick's mouth fell open.

"The Archeron River, the Darvaza gas crater, Mount Osore."

"You know a couple gateways into hell. So what?" He tried to laugh, and his face turned into a mask of agony. His little ponytail had come loose, his thin hair plastered to his head. He managed to prop himself into a sitting position against his bookshelf.

"What do you think happens when those bodies of water or the ones nearby are blessed by a gang of holy men?"

His slivery eyebrows lifted in surprise.

"Shit. I don't really know. You'd clap back like that, though?"

It came off as an overwhelming reprisal, even to her, but Mary figured it was a go-big-or go-home kind of situation. If she were making headway with the devil, she'd take it. She raised her gun again to register her certainty with him. His eyes went wide, the implied threat received.

"What do you want?" he asked.

"I want you to let Walker go."

"You just want me to give him to you?"

Mary shook her head. "No. *I* don't want him. You haven't been paying attention this whole time. I'm *divorcing* him. I want you to release him into his own custody."

The devil made a pained face as if he were struggling to understand what Mary had just said to him. "Where…where should I put him?" His mouth was hanging open like he was out of breath.

"I don't know. On a corner somewhere." Mary thought about that for a second and decided she needed to be definite, or Walker would be released on a street corner right as a semi-truck jumped a curb or a drive-by happened. "Put him in the restroom of the McDonald's on Rochester Road in Troy. In an empty stall."

"Which one?" Dr. Rick asked. "There are two. The one on the corner of Rochester and Big Beaver or the one across the street from Century 21?"

"I don't know. Century 21!"

Dr. Rick's expression became more twisted, like he was cresting a particularly uncooperative shit. "Why don't you…Why don't you get up on my desk?"

"Why would I do that?" Mary asked.

"So I can rip that baby out of you."

The notion was ridiculous and strong at the same time. She felt a part of her wanting to get up there, lie back, and spread her legs.

No.

It felt like she'd had to shove herself back into her own body, and she saw she'd taken a step closer to his desk. Had her general misery and growing urge to pee not been so present at that particular moment, she might have been seduced.

"We can eat it together," Dr. Rick said. "Three hundred thirty degrees for about an hour forty. You can't beat the *crisp* on that *skin*."

Mary's mouth watered when she thought of the tender flesh, the juices exploding in her mouth and running down her throat—

"No!" she said aloud. "You're going to let him go, or this is going to get much, much worse for you."

His eyes went wider a moment, and then he closed them as if he were drowning in his own agony. "It will take time."

"No. Now!"

"It doesn't work like that," Dr. Rick said. "I may be the devil, but there's a whole machine to this thing. I give the command, and it has to go through all the...the...cogs and gears before it happens."

"How do I know you've done it?"

"It...it won't take long." Dr. Rick coughed up blood. "Oh, man. Could I have some water?"

"No. Not until I know Walker is out of hell."

"All right," Dr. Rick said. "Fair enough. What else you got in that purse, though? What would you have hit me with had I told you to fuck off after you gut shot me and put this thing on my chest?"

Mary smiled. Then she took out the handheld grater.

Dr. Rick's eyes bugged.

"Okay, okay, okay. Whatever you do, don't stick that thing up my ass."

Mary made a face at him and put the grater on his desk. She took out a tube of lip gloss.

"No, please," he said, looking at the tube in her hands. "Not up my ass. I'm begging you."

She applied the gloss and dropped it back into her purse. Then she fished around and took out her keys.

"Anything but that. Not keys! Not up my ass! Anything but that!"

He got on his hands and knees, aiming his ass in her direction. Mary dropped her keys back in her purse and zipped it closed. She was shocked, to say the least, until she reminded herself this was the devil.

"How do you give the command to let him go?" she asked.

"It...it just takes a phone call." Dr. Rick slowly crawled onto his office chair-ball, and Mary raised the gun to remind him not to try anything. He picked up the handset to his phone, thought a moment, then began pushing buttons. "It's ringing," he said.

They sat in silence for a full minute. Dr. Rick grimaced occasionally, his hand hovering over his gunshot wound. He rolled his eyes and pushed a button.

"Phone tree," he said.

He pushed a few more buttons, and Mary heard the polite female voice on the other end, though she couldn't make out what the woman was saying.

"Yeah, this is Dr. Rick. Bob Shea, please...Uh-huh." He waited another thirty seconds

before a…sound. It wasn't like a human voice or a
voice of any kind at all. It resembled a concrete
block being dragged over another concrete block.
"Hey, Bobby! How's it going?…Yeah? How's the
grandkids?…Oh, man. Time really flies, doesn't
it?…Yeah…Yeah." Dr. Rick sat back in his chair
and folded a leg. "Say, look, I need you to do
something for me. Yeah. Operation Kill Walker
Harris."

"You son of a—" Mary aimed at his head.

"Whoa! One sec, Bob." Dr. Rick put the
phone to his chest and looked at Mary, his face
waxen and gray. "No, you don't understand. That's
just what I called releasing him. I never intended to
do it, so it didn't matter what I named it. You gotta
trust me here!"

Mary wasn't sure what to do. She *didn't*
trust him, but she didn't see she had much of a
choice. Mary gave him the slightest of nods.

"Okay, Bob, I'm back. Yeah, you heard
right. OKWH. And I need it right away…Yeah, I
know it's gonna take a little bit, but I need you to
step on that as much as possible…All right, thanks.
Hey, how's that fine piece of an ex-wife of
yours?…Yeah, those *were* the days, weren't they?
Biggest three I ever saw…No-no. Not me. I'm a
promised man. Gettin' married today…Oh, in about
a half hour or so…Thanks. Talk to you soon."

Dr. Rick hung up.

"So, it's done?" Mary asked.

Dr. Rick nodded. "Absolutely. He should be
walking free in a couple hours. But you don't have
a couple hours, Mary. You're about to give birth."

"I think I can hang on for another two hours."

"Yeah, maybe. But you're going to be writhing in pain with contractions. Plus, you have eclampsia to worry about. Believe me, it's bad stuff. I looked it up on *WebMD*."

Heat rose into her face. Mary had heard the term before and knew it had something to do with high blood pressure during pregnancy. She had to admit to herself this part of her plan was a little foggy.

Her stomach rumbled, and Mary fished out another protein bar. She and Dr. Rick just stared at one another.

"Could I have that water now?" he asked, the corners of his dry lips white. "I'm so parched right now."

"I think you can hold a little longer," she said.

Blood had spread on his shirt to his beltline, just under his nipples. He looked terrible but sounded fine and didn't seem to be in as much pain as someone who had been gutshot should have been. Mary had had eyewitness experience to what that looked like, and this wasn't it.

"You know, Mary, despite me being...y'know, *me*, this is a mortal form, and it can be killed. While this body dying ultimately wouldn't prevent me from anything I want to do, it would be inconvenient to lose it. The least you could let me have is a cup of water so this body doesn't get too dehydrated."

"Okay." Mary nodded toward the water cooler behind him. "One cup."

Dr. Rick turned and wheeled over to the water cooler. He took one of the cone-shaped cups on top and filled it. The cooler glugged, a pocket of air bubbling to the top. He downed the cup, balled it into his fist, and let it drop to the floor. Dr. Rick sat back in his chair and blinked slowly several times.

"Better," he whispered. "You mind if we listen to my jam?"

Mary didn't see the harm. She nodded.

"Vladimir, play 'Candy Licker'." The Marvin Sease song began playing from a hockey-puck-shaped device on his desk. The sound was actually pretty good for such a small thing. "You should probably take a seat," Dr. Rick said. "All that standing isn't good for you, probably. I mean, I guess it's not. I'm not going to sleep. I'm just gonna close my eyes. If I start uttering phrases in any ancient languages, could you write them down? I'm doing a thing—putting together a chapbook. Just write down whatever you hear and spell the big stuff phonetically."

Dr. Rick was silent for several minutes.

"Well played, Mary. Well played." He put his head back and closed his eyes.

Mary was amazed he seemed to instantly fall asleep. She had the sensation of an impending contraction and kept her breathing as steady as possible. Her swollen feet ached. Mary pushed one of the chairs in front of the desk back a couple of feet and sat. She'd worn a pair of Nikes for better mobility but was now realizing the mistake. The shoes were like designer traps for her feet, considering all the water she was retaining. She should have worn her sandals. Barefoot would have been better than this.

Mary hesitated but decided taking off her shoes would be worth it. Her feet thumped with relief, and she closed her eyes long enough to enjoy the freedom. Then she sat upright and aimed at Dr. Rick, who hadn't moved an inch.

He hadn't moved. An inch.

She watched his chest for a long moment, and it didn't rise or fall. Dammit, was he dead?

Mary stood, the feeling of a hundred pinpricks in the soles of her feet. "Dr. Rick?" she said, leaning over the table.

Him dying definitely was not a part of her plans, and satan or not, if his mortal form were dead, there was enough DNA evidence for her to wind up in handcuffs.

"Dr. Rick?" she said again. "Are you okay?" His almost half-blood-soaked shirt was answer enough to her question. She approached him like a sleeping bear, creeping around the desk to get a closer look. It didn't seem like he was breathing. His skin was pale, but he hadn't been exactly tan before.

She slicked one hand down her dress to dry her palm as much as she could. Then she reached for his neck, finally placing two fingers where the big pulse should have been. Mary waited. And waited. It was almost a full minute before she gave in to the fact before her.

Dr. Rick was dead.

"Shit," she said.
His face cracked. Then his jaw fell off.
"*Shit*," she said again.

Chapter 24. All the Murderers in Heaven

This wasn't the first time Alfred had been afraid. There'd been a handful of times over the hundred-plus years he'd been alive. But all of those had been when he was *alive*. Now he was dead, *in heaven*, and was absolutely terrified.

Unless he was misreading the situation, which he doubted, god had been murdered in this underground chamber, leaving the inmates to run the asylum. The angels—all gone, as far as Hammercock could tell after returning from a reconnaissance—couldn't give him the answers he wanted, and Alfred wondered if they were responsible for the deicide.

But the chamber held all kinds of goodies: bejeweled goblets, weapons with odd handholds which had been wielded by creatures only to be described as alien, texts whispering in foreign tongues while he turned their pages, and wood.

Not just any wood, Alfred realized upon examining the pieces. He was suspicious of the large, square-headed nails and how the remnants fit into one another to make a post and crossbar, but the letters carved into the post settled it.

"INRI," Alfred said with a superior smile on his face.

"What?" Hammercock asked.

"And they said *I* was the heretic." Alfred laid a hand on his chest. "Iesus Nazarenus Rex Iudaeorum. Jesus of Nazarene, King Jew. Behold, the remnants of the means of execution of the one

who died for all our sins and how I plan to put a
thumb in the eye of heaven. Help me with this."

Morgan was the only one spry enough to
climb out of the chamber. They'd wound up having
to make a rope out of their tunics, having him pull
them out one by one. Alfred had elected not to put
his tunic back on—everything about him would be
as much an affront as possible.

Morgan seemed to be rousing from his
stupor. Alfred wondered if it had been a temporary
effect of the fountains.

And then he began humping a tree.

Alfred had his idea, though. Originally, his
intent had been to kill someone in heaven, but
considering that had already been done, he needed
to switch it up.

And what Mary had done to him gave him
an idea.

"Hammercock," he said.

"Yes, angel?"

"Are you sure *all* the angels are gone?"

Chapter 25. Dearly Beloved, Friends, and Sponsors

Okay. Median knew the tune, but he couldn't quite place it. Satan danced down the aisle to a live band playing an upbeat, horn-heavy song Median was pretty sure was from a movie. The band had a sign above them that read "Swingin' Fireballs," but he'd never heard of them. Median looked at satan again. He had a blue police strobe light on his head, and it clicked—that was the theme song from the movie *The Naked Gun.*

He looked at the sign again and wondered if "Swingin' Fireballs" was just some cover band or if they were the ones who'd originally made it. Now he was paying attention, there were a lot of signs around. Up on the mezzanine, a sign hung off the side that read: "Mezzanine brought to you by Brad's Pelts." To either side of the entrance doors was a sign, one for PedroCorps, whatever that was, and the other for Very Good Meat Foods. That last one sounded suspect. Along one wall was a sign either written in kanji or some language not of this Earth, and on the other side was "Martha's Slaptastic Mince Pie."

Satan danced his way closer, and Median made out something printed on the lane of carpeting the devil was on. "Kejuan Inman Loves Leilani," he read aloud. He looked at the pastor, master of ceremonies, or whatever the guy standing at the top of the stairs next to him was. "Is this whole thing sponsored?"

The man wore a kente cloth around his neck, although Median was relatively sure he wasn't black. He definitely wasn't white, but his facial features were just bland enough, his skin just olive enough, to be one of a dozen or so ethnicities. He was bald down to a lack of eyebrows. The narrow spectacles tamped the look of feral surprise, considering his hung-open mouth, and it appeared his teeth were pointed.

"*Shh*," the man said, putting a finger to his lips. He didn't have fingernails, but actual nails instead.

Finally, the devil made it to the foot of the stairs, and Median wasn't surprised when he took a knee right there instead of simply coming up and assuming his place. It was his wedding, but it appeared he was going to make absolutely certain he was the center of attention.

The horns played the end of the song, holding their last note while they faded. A single, trailing note from an organ rose, stretching for an interminable thirty seconds. The devil remained on his knee with his head hung low. He'd gone full satan, with his skin red and two yellow horns about twice the length of Median's index fingers, half as thick as his wrist.

"Dearly beloved, we are gathered here today in celebration of the union of two magnificent souls."

The voice was definitely a reverend's—the kind Median had grown up hearing in baptist churches. It was coming from unseen speakers, and he glanced around until he spotted the man in black and red robes, complete with crosses and that sash thing over his neck. He had on big square-framed glasses and had short, fuzzy, salt and pepper hair. His skin was the color of coffee with a liberal amount of cream. Median recognized the man suspended from the ceiling in what looked like a golden birdcage.

It was Reverend Fawkes.

He'd been the preacher at his grandmother's church when Median was little. Median recalled the man had battled cancer and won. Not long after his return, he'd had to step down because he'd no longer been able to keep up with his pastoral duties and work a full-time job. Apparently, the pastor's crushing medical debt had forced him into the private sector.

Despite never really caring for church, Median had always liked the reverend because, away from the pulpit, he seemed like an actual human being Median could relate to. Median had gone on a few boys' weekend retreats with the man, and despite how such a thing had gone wrong in many other situations, the reverend—Big Kev, as he was affectionately called away from church—had always been a fun hang.

So what the hell was he doing in hell?

Median had stopped going to church a long time ago. Big Kev had probably been the only thing worth considering being a Christian. He really had been one of the good guys. If Big Kev had died, why wasn't *he,* of all people, in heaven?

"It's been a long time comin'," Reverend Fawkes sang in that almost-end-of-service-oh-thank-god tone familiar to anyone with service in a baptist church. "They said he's been sinnin' since the beginnin'—hah! They said he prowls around like a roaring lion, seeking lambs to devour—hah! They said he has nothing to do with the truth. But I say the truth is, he didn't enslave the Jews! The truth is, he didn't leave with no clues! The truuuuuuuth is, he didn't write the rules. Oh lord, I wish somebody was listenin'!"

Median noticed the crowd in the pews for the first time, and for the most part, they were unremarkable. Human in appearance, mostly, in church-going attire, getting riled up as the reverend sermonized, pumping fists in the air, waving hands in mock-surrender, chiming in with "Yes!" and "Yessir!" Several people stood up, including one man who just continuously clapped his hands with the biggest frown on his face.

The organ was belting out exclamation points with each sentence the reverend sang. His birdcage was almost lowered to the floor, and the organ began belting out notes with the growl of each word. "Liar! Deceiver! Thief! Murderer! Snake! Enemy! Destrooooooooooooooooyer!"

The crowd was really wound up. Someone shouted, "All right now!" when Reverend Fawkes mopped the corners of his brow with a folded cream-colored handkerchief, as if his whole face wasn't drenched with sweat.

He went on with several more choice descriptors for the father of lies, finally concluding with: "Husband." The organ went crazily up and down the scale, and the birdcage opened right when it rested on the floor.

Reverend Fawkes walked up behind satan and bent, laying a hand on his back. "Today, we mark the end of Seven."

The way he said it sounded like "seven" should have been capitalized, to Median's ears. It rang a distant bell, but the reverend would have to fill in the gaps.

"At the end of every seven years, you shall grant a re*lease* of debts. And O father, hasn't it been seven and seven and seven and seven and seven and seven and seven…"

The man with the kente cloth over his neck turned and left. Median wondered if he was going to get something or—

"Today marks the end because this is a new beginning."

The organ had come down from its frenzied piping and now was playing softly in the background. Reverend Fawkes took the three steps up and assumed the other man's place on the platform.

He smiled, nodded to Median, and then said, "Arise and behold your bride."

The organ promptly began playing "Here Comes the Bride," and the devil stood, taking his place on the dais as well. The birdcage quickly lifted into the ceiling, and soft white light flooded from the doorway. Two figures emerged from the light. One had to have been *her,* but he was stymied as to who would be walking her down the aisle. It turned out to be some rando older white guy, probably her father, Median guessed. The man looked frightened, but his strides were steady, walking arm in arm with her down the aisle.

Beatricia was just as ravishing as every other time he'd ever seen her. He'd definitely loved Mary and been attracted to her, but he couldn't recall being as turned on by any woman as much as he was the one before him right now. A few people were standing while she proceeded down the aisle, and an older woman in all white and a giant hat seemed to have fainted with her eyes open.

Median puzzled over whether or not the woman was dead, when there was a huge explosion.

"They're here," the devil said. "A little early, but whatever." He was smiling and suddenly had a trident in his hand. "Everyone get ready," he called to the people and demons in the pews.

The people armed themselves with a whole host of different weapons. From sub-machine guns, to spears, to maces on chains. The woman who had fainted still hadn't moved, but people stepped over her. Beatricia had pulled a broadsword seemingly from nowhere and pushed the man escorting her aside.

"Let's go kill some angels," the devil said.

Chapter 26. Double Shit

So Dr. Rick had pretty much broken into about a hundred pieces, and those pieces were breaking down into flakes and the flakes into a fine powder. Mary had been expecting him to get up at any moment, to rise from his own ashes, but he just…died.

But that didn't mean she was out of danger. About a moment after he'd begun falling into a neat pile, the whole building had been rocked. Mary had at first thought it was connected to him apparently dying, but then the screaming had started.

There was the distant sound of glass breaking followed by the scrambling of feet. Mary hadn't known what to make of what was going on until she'd seen the big silhouette pass by the door.

Okay, even then she didn't know what to make of it. Especially considering the figure seemed to have wings. She guessed it had been an angel, but she had no clue what one would have been doing here.

So she'd killed the devil. It had seemed way too easy, but whatever. Mary could compartmentalize and deal with that later. Something more dangerous was going on just outside this office. Somebody screamed, and a moment later, red squirted across the frosted glass.

Thick blue liquid slashed across the window. Mary had a guess what that was, but something lethal enough to kill an angel was more than she was capable of dealing with. She needed to get out of this room but wasn't sure how.

Mary spotted the phone on the desk. She picked up the handset and put it to her ear. Mary was reaching for the buttons when she realized there was no dial tone, jiggling the plungers a couple of times just to be sure.

She laid the handset down, remembering her cell phone. Mary had no idea why that hadn't come to mind first, but she dug into her purse and pulled it out. The face was cracked, but she risked slicing her fingertips, swiping to unlock it. It took several tries before she was able to put in her code, and as soon as the home screen appeared, random apps began opening. She struggled in vain to close them and finally had to lock her phone again when a delivery app began an order she couldn't back out of.

Mary thought about trying the desk phone again, even though she knew better. She really could use Derek right now, but how would she reach him? Wait, he was a god. And how did someone speak to a god?

She bowed her head and muttered what was at the top of her mind.

"God, I hate him so much, and I know I shouldn't love him still. I should just turn around now and walk away. He deserves everything. All of the bad. It's on him. But please, let me see this through. Let me see my baby."

Glass shattered somewhere in the hall, and she knelt behind the desk. It was probably a miracle that whatever was going on out there hadn't come bursting in here, but she didn't think she could count on that for long.

Something liquid and hot poured down between thighs. On instinct, Mary reached, even though she knew what it was. A contraction followed, as if to put an exclamation point on the whole thing, but this one was probably the strongest yet.

"Derek! Goddammit, I need you here right now!"

The glass in the door shattered, spraying the wall inches above her head. She peeked over the desk when the door was wrenched off its hinges. Heavy footfalls crunched broken glass on the floor. Mary didn't know if all the fighting outside had ceased or if her ears were ringing. She could *feel* whoever it was, he was so big. And then she saw a pair of sandaled feet.

She was hesitant to look up, but she had no intention of dying on her knees if death was the only thing on offer. Mary grabbed the corner of the desk and pulled herself into a standing position, nose-to-torso with this massive person.

"I'm dressed up like a woman for you," Derek said, and Mary tilted her head all the way back to look at her fiancé, who was almost bumping his head on the ceiling. He'd been big before, but now he was…Gigantic didn't seem word enough. He smiled, his teeth like white tombstones in his mouth. "I'm kidding. The Dahomey were guards of kings and queens, and I am a forward-thinking demi-god. How may I serve you, my love?"

Save for the sandals and a modest brown cloth skirt, Derek was nude, his bulging muscles the bulgiest she'd ever seen them. He had a curved sword with a tip like it could double as a giant bottle opener and a spear with a short blade, like it was made of bone. Mary thought the light was reflecting off his dark skin, but he actually had a swath of white paint across his forehead.

"I...I..." she began, stymied to see him like this.

"Mary, there is a great deal I did not tell you about me. I was afraid, but I cannot excuse my obfuscation. I may be half-god, but you are the strongest part of me, and it would pain me to lose you." He knelt and took her hand, still more than half a head taller than her, covering it with his other after he propped the spear against the wall. "I am sorry."

"Okay." She smiled. Mary's anger at him was a distant memory. She shook off her surprise, trying to wrap her mind around how she was going to say this to him. He already thought of the life inside her as his own, even though he had to have known it wasn't. "I need you to do something for me."

"I would lay waste to a *nation* of your enemies. Men, women, even children."

She had no doubt he meant what he said by his determined expression.

"Well, no. I don't need that much. I just need you to clear a path so I can get upstairs."

He nodded, staring at her with a near maniacal gleam in his eyes.

"What?"

"You are mine, woman. But you have to complete your journey. The legba pursuing you will not stop until you have dealt with it." He put a massive hand over her belly. "Bring our baby home safe. Free your husband."

She narrowed her own eyes. "Do you know?"

"I know everything. You intend on walking into almost certain death, ready to reach into the maw of evil and tear out its heart. I love you even more because of it." He stood, the tiny cloth covering his crotch barely hiding his huge erection. Derek picked up his spear and walked toward the doorway. "I would take you now if it wouldn't hurt the child."

Hell, the child? Mary was certain he'd break her pelvis if they had sex right now.

"I am not threatened by your Walker Harris. I'm a demi-god. What can he do better than me?"

Mary shrugged. "Make sure you come home too."

He looked over his shoulder and smiled at her. "Please. It's been a long time since I gave an angel a whipping. This will be fun!"

Derek charged out into the hall, and Mary froze in shock for just a moment when he skewered a charging angel with his spear, lifting it up to the ceiling while he laughed. He was so big but so *fast*. Derek stopped, the angel on his spear continuing his momentum, flying off and into another angel. A man holding what looked like an ornate table leg with nails jutting out of it swung at Derek, but Derek drew his sword in a blur and slashed through the man's forearms and torso. He spun around and threw his spear in her direction. It thudded into the chest of a woman, pinning her to the wall two feet away from Mary.

Derek waved her forward, his spear extracting itself from the woman's corpse and flying back to his hand. Mary was past the point of trying to disguise the pain she was in, but Derek made no mention of it when he slowed his pace to match hers. They proceeded down the hall littered with bodies of humans, angels, and monsters the likes she'd never seen in her life, reaching the door to the stairwell.

"She is up there, alone." Derek looked confused. "A woman who is dead yet still lingers somewhere in the in-between?" He shook his head. Then he leaned over and kissed her. He opened the door for her and Mary went in. A second later, he was screaming like a wild man, taking on what appeared to be a giant, pink tentacle.

Mary immediately fell to her knees. She didn't know how she was going to do this. Mary was tired, in pain, and a baby was about to come out of her. But she still had to fight an evil aligned with the devil, who had promised to kill her child.

She had a sense it was powerful, but running from it would only allow it to gain even more strength when it finally found her. It had to be now. And it had to be Mary who dealt with it.

She recalled Derek looking uncomfortable in the Lamaze class and all but running out of the room. Mary didn't understand why. Maybe feminine energy was required, or maybe it was his god-ness excluding him from interceding— whatever it was, she accepted this as her fight. Mary didn't have to try to rescue Walker. That had been her own guilt motivating her. She was a big girl and had made this shit sandwich herself. It was time to take a big ol' bite.

"Get on your feet, dammit." Despite wanting to lie down, Mary got on her knees and grabbed the railing. She pulled until she was on her feet somehow and looked up at the stairs. "Baby steps…baby steps."

She stared at the first one in front of her, telling herself it wasn't a mile high. Her mother had been a carpenter, and Mary had had to be with her many times when she'd been building a new house, putting on an addition, or many of the odd jobs she'd taken. Mary recalled rise over run for a main stair—8¼ inches over 9 inches.

Eight inches.

All she needed to do was lift her foot eight inches. If she couldn't do as little as that, she might as well go home now. She didn't care if it was by force of will or magic, but her foot lifted from the floor and placed lightly on the run of the step. Mary took a deep breath, as if she had just hefted a mighty stone and moved it a long distance. Her other foot joined the first.

That didn't seem to have been so bad. Mary was all set to congratulate herself, when she saw the rest of the flight of stairs staring back at her.

"Shitty shit, shit-shit," she said.

Chapter 27. To Catch an Angel

Assembling the execution device had been simple. Alfred had surmised not *all* the angels had left. The idea of heaven being unguarded didn't make sense to him, and it was just a matter of finding where one of them was. Considering how horny they'd almost all been, luring one out into the open wouldn't be too difficult.

Alfred had always been beautiful by anyone's measurement. Women and men had fallen in love with him on sight. He'd been with so many he'd stopped bothering to count. Alfred guessed the name of the angel revealing itself to him before it had spoken.

Pravuil.

"Do you desire me?" Alfred had asked.

Pravuil had not spoken, simply nodding his head and following while Alfred led it through the city. They'd reached the Soup of Life and the execution device made from the cross used in the crucifixion of Jesus.

"Come down here with me," Alfred said to the angel.

It looked at him, lust and confusion in its eyes.

"I must not," Pravuil said. "I am a scribe of god."

"I'll give you something worth writing about."

The angel began descending and was about a few feet away when a fireball shot across the sky.

They all saw it, and Pravuil lifted higher, quill and tablet suddenly in hand. Alfred swore, his plans dashed, but even he was curious what this was.

It raced away from them, then abruptly changed directions, zig-zagging, its flaming tail leaving star-shaped afterimages in Alfred's eyes. It seemed to course-correct and began coming their way.

Alfred was fascinated, so he didn't think of the potential danger.

"Angel," Hammercock said, grabbing his shoulder. "We need to move."

The two men began running in the direction of the fireball, anticipating it overshooting them. He didn't know whether or not Morgan followed. It zipped overhead, the heat from the fireball trailing past running a chill through Alfred, and he realized they'd left his execution device.

Alfred turned around and tried to run back. He'd made it two steps, when the fireball crashlanded into the hill, destroying it.

He fell to his knees and roared like a beast at the sky. God—if such a creature did exist—was a bastard for waiting until the penultimate moment to thwart him. There was no reason for this to have happened, except to put a finger in his eye.

"This isn't heaven." Alfred shook his head. "This is just another hell. Everything is hell. A latticework of hells, an infinite sprig of hells…grown rich and full from the dark soil of the heart. There is no heaven. Heaven is truly no longer having to exist."

"Angel!" Hammercock said, stepping ahead of him.

Alfred looked to where he was pointing. At the center of the flames, something began rising. It was big, and it wasn't until it emerged from the fire that Alfred could make it out as human in shape.

It was the big angel, big by their standards—Gamael. He walked out of the fire casually, as if his flesh weren't burning. But he was anything but unmarred. His armor was either missing or dented and broken. One of his eyes had been scored, and his mouth was half swollen. One arm terminated in a ragged wrist, flesh hanging in blue ribbons. He had wide claw marks running diagonally across his chest, and he limped like one of his legs was broken.

Alfred kept waiting for the wounds to begin knitting closed or for his hand to grow back. Hammercock's injury had been much more extreme, and even he'd been mostly healed in a few minutes' time. But the farther the angel walked, the more Alfred was surprised to see his injuries remaining.

A glint of light flashed off something between them, and Alfred realized it was at least a piece of the blade he'd used in his execution device. While Pravuil wasn't a warrior, he was intact, whereas Gamael under normal circumstances could probably do much more damage than Penemue and Kochab had done to Hammercock.

But this wasn't a normal circumstance.

213

Yes, he was standing despite horrific injury, but he had to be weakened. If he were ever vulnerable, now was the time.

Morgan ran alongside Gamael, and the giant angel swatted him away. That also bothered Alfred. At some point, he'd begun to think of the buffoon as his and didn't like seeing him abused in such a manner. Morgan got up but was in his path, cowering while Gamael approached.

"*Him*," Alfred said. "We sacrifice him."

Hammercock didn't wait for further instruction, running straight for the big angel and flinging himself at him, hunching his body so he hit shoulder first. He succeeded in stopping the angel's forward momentum, but not much else. Gamael swung his arm like a hammer but must have misjudged the distance without his hand, almost toppling over when he missed Hammercock.

The old man took advantage of them being momentarily at eye level with each other and punched him right in the empty eye socket. Alfred took his eyes off the pair and ran in the general direction of the blade. He spotted it and pushed his body even harder. It was a long piece of blade, and he pinched it as best he could in his hands, trying to pull it from the firm earth.

Both sides were sharp, and he managed to knick himself without even realizing he'd touched an edge. It was painless, and that gave him an idea of how sharp it still was. Alfred chanced a look over his shoulder. Hammercock was on his back, Gamael poised over him to strike. The old man was unnaturally quick and rolled away just as the angel struck.

Alfred cursed himself he'd decided to forego his robes, realizing he was going to have to bleed a lot before he got this blade. He took a couple of deep breaths, steeling himself before he wrapped his hand around it and pulled. This time, he *did* feel the edge cut into him, splitting through flesh until it stopped at bone. This certainly wasn't the worst pain Alfred had ever felt, but it had its own unique intensity.

He continued pulling until the blade finally budged. It was just a little, and he didn't withhold his cry of agony. Alfred was sure the blade had begun cutting into bone. Blood trailed down the blade ,and he felt a moment's light-headedness, his extremities cold like he'd thrust them in ice water.

Then Morgan was there, steadying him with one hand, his other on the blade, their blood commingling while they pulled together. It moved ever so slightly more, like the earth was starting to give way. The idiot's grin on Morgan's face was a bit sobering for Alfred. He was certain this was the most intense amount of pain he'd ever felt. The blade sliced through a quarter of Morgan's hand, cleaving off his thumb and a significant chunk of meat, which dangled by a string of flesh from his wrist.

"Angel!" Hammercock said behind him, but Alfred forced himself to ignore the man's call.

The blade was loosening. They reversed their grips and began to push back up. He knew a

215

moment later why Hammercock had called out to him.

The steps of the angel came closer.

Morgan had the benefit of seeing Gamael's approach. But he never lost that blank smile on his face, never seemed to worry. Alfred wrapped his hand around the blade and tried to pull it, succeeding in cutting into his hand until his pinky and ring fingers fell off. He made the pain as distant as he could and tried to regrip.

Something about Morgan's eyes—

The other man had stopped smiling, when he let go of the blade and gave Alfred a mighty shove, sending him tumbling backward. But the blade was poised under his chest, just as Gamael's fist came down where Alfred's head had been and where Morgan's back now was. He might have already pierced himself with the blade before the blow connected, but the result was immediate and definitive.

The blade slid through Morgan until he hit the ground, cutting through him like a knife through the breast of a Thanksgiving turkey. But Gamael had also skewered himself, the blade piercing through his wrist.

He tried to wrench his arm back, but the agony must have been too intense. Blue blood sprayed from his wound, and Gamael lifted his face skyward and screamed.

It was the sound of absolute destruction.

Alfred fell to the ground, covering his ears in pain. Gamael's scream went on for an incalculable length of time, until Alfred's curses

were overwhelmed and he thought he had lost
consciousness.

When he dared to remove his hands and
open his eyes, his vision pulsed in red for a few
heartbeats before returning to normal. Alfred stood,
looking at something that shouldn't have been, but
still somehow was.

They were both stone, truly dead so far as
Alfred could see, but that wasn't the remarkable
part.

Somehow, Morgan had gotten on top—well,
behind Gamael—the angel's tunic still in place as
he gripped Gamael by the hips, that beatific smile
back on his face.

Chapter 28. The Devil's Best Feature

"Man, I should be out there *kickin'* ass!" the devil said, pacing back and forth.

Two enormous demon bodyguards stood at opposite ends of the room. Median sat in front of the mirror facing satan, who was chastising himself with false bravado.

"I bet I'd kill like thirty angels, all in like two minutes." He punched a wall and hissed in pain, shaking his fist.

"Why don't you just go out there, then?" Median dared to ask.

The devil flashed a glance at him and continued his pacing. "Because…" he said.

That had never been an allowable excuse when Median had used it as a child, and the answer emboldened him. "Because why?"

"Because BB won't let me, okay?" the devil shouted. "She said I might get hurt."

In the hubbub and hustle ending in Median being roughly ushered into this changing room with the devil and two enormous bodyguards armed with melee weapons, he had noticed Beatricia had made no move to retreat. She'd dived right into the fighting. As beautiful as he'd found her every other time he'd seen her, she was absolutely angelic, tearing into the abdomen of an angel, disemboweling him before leaping and gouging out his eyes.

"Where…where did those angels come from?" Median asked.

"Man, this is hell. Technically, I run it, but who do you think *owns* it?"

"Oh."

"Yeah. I don't know where they got in, but I've always presumed they could come in anywhere they wanted. Anyway, we were expecting them."

"You were? Why?"

"BB had this idea." The devil sighed. "That our wedding could be such an affront that the angels wouldn't allow it. That as soon as they heard about it, they would be planning an attack."

"Okay, but...so?"

"It's this whole thing...BB can explain it a lot better than I could. She called it some sort of reconciliation between heaven and hell." He twirled his hands around each other.

Median definitely wasn't going to be able to make sense of her plan, but a light bulb came on. It was *her* plan. Not the devil's.

"Did you propose to her, or did she propose to you?"

"What?" The devil finally looked at Median. "The fuck you talkin' about? I proposed to her. Of course, I did."

Something about his answer came off as defensive to Median. He recalled a conversation between him and Mary about how he'd approached her to ask her out years before, and she'd wound up telling him *she'd* given him the signal first. Median had had conversations with other women, especially on porn sets, about how they'd given "the signal" to alert a man she wanted to go out with him. He didn't understand, but he understood it was a thing he didn't understand.

"You two met here? I mean, at St. Elo?"

There was a loud boom, and the walls of the room shook, dust cascading from the ceiling.

"Yeah, of course. I mean, there's a strict hands-off policy so far as dating between employees and upper management, but y'know, there's only so long a guy can take a beautiful woman making googly eyes at him. Besides, I *am* Mr. Fleas."

Median had never heard that particular name before, but he was starting to get an idea that "the signal" had been in play here. That would mean, though, Beatricia hadn't been the innocent he'd originally thought she was. That she'd been the man behind the curtain.

But wait, this *s the devil talking.* How could Median believe anything *he* said?

"What did she say that attracted her to you?" Median asked.

"Come on. I'm the devil." He stopped pacing and held out his arms. "What feature am I best known for?"

"Horns?"

"No."

"Flawless red skin?"

"Oo—thank you. But no."

"Goat legs?"

"*No!*" The devil huffed in annoyance. Then he smiled comically wide and pointed with both index fingers at his open mouth. "My smile? Come on. In every depiction you've ever seen of me, the pearly whites are always poppin'! I be flossin' and everything!"

"Oh."

The devil's face fell, and he reached up to touch his horns. "You think people really notice my *horns* more? You don't think they're too big, do you? Or too small?"

Median had no idea how to answer. But he was sure he was being manipulated. The devil wasn't the one in control here. It was his soon-to-be wife.

"So what is the plan exactly, with me here?" Median asked.

"I told you. We needed a living human to take part in our nuptials."

"You don't need to sacrifice me or eat me?"

"No. We don't *need* to. If I'm being honest, the appeal for me was making Mary toil for that baby. You gotta know, I don't give a shit about you one way or another. I could have two dozen living people down here anytime I want. Hell, I could have. One per penis. And souls?" The devil rolled his eyes.

"I get it. You don't need any more souls."

"The only reason I still take them is because I have a mandate. To keep the doors open, the doors can never close."

Median noticed the exhaustion in his eyes.

"Why don't you get out?" he asked.

The devil looked questioningly at him, as if he hadn't understood.

"No, for real. Why don't you just *leave*?"

221

"Well, I don't know about all that." Satan looked around nervously.

The devil casually waved a hand through the air, and Median felt a slight pressure on his eyes and chest. It was gone an instant later, and when he looked around, nothing had changed.

Nothing. Had. Changed.

The room seemed to have frozen. The guards, who had been like statues before, now had a stillness about them akin to death.

"So, tell me more about this 'getting out'." The devil made air quotes around the last two words.

Median couldn't tell if he was being facetious. He couldn't imagine the devil hadn't thought about escaping hell, but then again, he'd been programmed to believe there were multiple devils when—if Median could believe the old guy they'd met at that school's gymnasium—there was only one. Could it be possible satan was also programmed to not be able to fathom escaping being who he was?

Median supposed that could have been the case. There was just so much up in the air, and Median couldn't take any of it for granted. He wasn't even sure he believed the battle going on outside.

"Well, you said it yourself," Median began. "You have all kinds of bodies up there you can assume. I'm guessing you can pretty much do that anytime you want. Right?"

"True."

"So why not just take over one of them and just *not* come back?"

Satan drew away like he'd been struck in the face. "Say that again?"

Median thought he'd said it pretty clearly. "Why not take over one of your other bodies and not come back to hell?"

The devil stared at him and blinked several times. "I'm not getting it. One mo' 'gin."

"I'm going to try something. Bear with me." Median leaned forward and grabbed the devil by the shoulders.

Despite being the devil and all that implied, he was a relatively small guy. Maybe five four and a hundred forty pounds at most. Median was no giant by any means, but he didn't need to stand up to reach.

"Repeat after me," Median said.

Satan nodded.

"Take over one of my bodies…"

"Take over one of my bodies…"

"And don't come back."

"And don't come back." The devil blinked a couple of times. "Wait, what?"

"Man, somebody's got their hand up your ass to the shoulder, don't they?"

Median let him go.

The room shuddered, followed by a prolonged scream from outside the room. Whatever the devil had done to stop everything had stopped…stopping. Then the door to the room opened.

"You ready to get married?" a smiling, ichor-soaked Beatricia asked, swiping blue gore from her face.

Chapter 29. Like Sam & Diane

Median wasn't relatively sure it was his turn. At some point, he was going to be brought back in the chapel, but they were seating the surviving guests. He couldn't tell, but there seemed to be more of them than before, even though there were…parts of demons strewn about, along with humans and angels.

Several of the demons were eyeing him, and Median was certain if he weren't some important part of the ceremonies, they would have him as an *amuse-gueule*.

The one currently giving him a dead-eye stare looked like an onyx-skinned shark with legs and a dorsal ring of thumb-sized, triangular, yellow bony-looking horns. It had on a white suit with a bow tie and was surrounded by three smaller versions of it—that were still larger than Median—without the horns, or whatever they were.

A thing bumped into him, and Median turned to see it was nothing more than a grouping of tentacles all waving straight in the air. He didn't see eyes or a mouth, reaching to brush off the slime it had smeared on his suit jacket sleeve.

"I wouldn't touch that if I were you," a thing said to him. This particular demon looked like an anvil with arms and legs. "You'll juice yourself to death."

"Juice?" Median didn't like the sound of that, but didn't know what it meant.

"Every fluid that can come out of your body will come out until you're essentially a mummy.

It'll take forever before the poison runs its course through you."

Median was about to point out it hadn't said it would kill him, then remembered he was in hell. This creature probably assumed he was already dead or immortal, or whatever *it* was. The anvil demon produced a handkerchief from an inner pocket of its jacket.

"Allow me." It swiped at the wet spot until he'd removed most of the stuff, carefully folded the handkerchief, then placed it in his mouth.

"Whoa! I thought you said—"

"That isn't the same issue for me as it is for you." Its raisin eyes bulged. "Uh, excuse me. I have to use the restroom."

Median had no way of knowing for certain, but he was relatively sure the sudden protrusion on its upper back was some sort of erection.

There was security at the entrance of the chapel proper. They had cleared the remains of everyone and everything who had died inside— mostly by throwing whatever body parts out here— and were seating guests again.

As far as Median could tell, it had been a trap. The angels had invaded and given a good accounting of themselves but had been overwhelmed by a force lying in wait for them. He had no idea how far the fighting had spread and could only guess the number of "good guys" who had died was a lot. Body parts were strewn about— more wings than anything—and feathers were plastered everywhere. He spotted a thin demon that had black and silver skin walking around with a

spear, jabbing the torsos of fallen angels that had to
have been inert, if dead weren't an actual thing
here.

There was an angel by the wall with four
demons surrounding it, moving still. His legs had
been torn off, his entrails spilling out behind him.
His wings looked severely broken. Most of the
feathers had been ripped away, and a fistful had
been stuffed into his mouth and pasted to his face in
ichor.

"Mercy," he said, after spitting out a bloody
clump of feathers, dragging himself with his one
good arm. "Kill me." His eyes had been gouged out,
the burst bulbs like exotic plants draping down his
cheeks.

Another demon stepped forward, quickly
knelt, cut off his nose, and pocketed it. The angel
must have been in so much agony, the additional
pain didn't seem to register.

Median eventually made it to the doors, but
security turned him away.

"You can't come in this entrance," the
demon said. It had the general shape of a man,
except it was flayed of skin and was all exposed
muscle and tendon. "You have to use the back
entrance."

Median didn't know his way around here.
Everywhere he'd gone, he'd been led or pushed in a
wheelchair. He made a show of looking around.
"Where is that?"

The demon rolled his eyes. "Around *back*."
He summarily dismissed Median by glancing past

him to the next demon in line and waving them forward.

Median was roughly shuffled to the middle of the room until the rest of the demons had been admitted, and then the doors were shut. He was alone, except for the janitor who appeared to be cleaning up the blood with a bucket and a mop made out of human hair still attached to a scalp. This one appeared human, wearing blue corduroy overalls and a matching fiddler's cap. He had a blond handlebar mustache, but other than that, there wasn't anything significant about him.

Median looked around for the critically injured angel. Someone must have removed him too—there was only a puddle of blue blood where he'd been.

"Pardon me." The janitor slopped the bloody scalp mop over his shoes.

Median jumped back with revulsion and held his tongue before he could say something reproachful. Bad enough the guy was already in hell. He didn't need some nobody yelling at him to boot.

The janitor kicked the wheeled bucket, rolling it his way. He mopped closer. "You ready to get outta here?" he seemed to ask the floor.

"Excuse me?" Median asked.

"Keep your voice down." The janitor raised his head and made a second's worth of eye contact.

"Holy—" Median immediately glanced around, realizing he'd spoken way too loud. He lowered his tone to a whisper. "Vinny, you're alive?"

a lowercase hell

"Rumors of my demise were premature." He
pronounced the last word with a hard "T". "I always
wanted to say that. Sorry about your feet, there.
Some seltzer water should take that right out." He
lowered his voice to a whisper. "My death was a
ruse. To make sure nobody was paying attention to
me when it was time to bone out."

"So that wasn't your skin? I mean, I thought
for sure you were…y'know."

"Oh, that was one of my skins," he said.
"Had to be as real as possible. I had to trade a favor
to make it happen."

Median didn't have the mental capacity to
unpack the horror of a demon having multiple
human skins it could wear like different outfits. But
the thought made him shudder.

"You had to do a favor for somebody for
them to rip your skin off?" Median asked, not
understanding. "What was the favor?"

Vinny looked up at him again, his eyes
wide. "You don't wanna know."

Median assumed he wasn't going to
continue when he looked back down.

"The window wiper, Jamie—she was able to
manage the skinning thing."

Median recalled seeing Vinny's skin being
used to scrub the windows, although he had trouble
thinking of "Jamie" as a singular entity. She had to
have been *huge*.

"Let's just say, they have seventeen vaginas
and eleven penises, and I had to get every single
one of them off. My armpits are sorer than any

229

other part of me. I couldn't even make a fist until yesterday, and it still hurts to blink."

Median didn't know what more could have been said and couldn't compute what he could have done. He wanted to thank Vinny for his service, but right then, whatever words he could have spoken seemed trivial.

"I'm sorry," Median said.

"Sorry?" The corner of Vinny's mouth curled up. "What for? That was the second best seven hours of my life. We're going steady now."

He mopped his way over to the doors exiting this room and dropped the mop back in the bucket. The room was still a mess, but there was so much about St. Elo that was unclean, Median thought it would hardly stand out.

They pushed down a long hallway, and he thought he had a good idea of where they were but still wasn't confident in his ability to navigate to the entrance from here. They entered the lobby area, and there was the delightful and slightly chubby Maddy, splayed over the counter, dead, her hand clutched around a fistful of feathers.

Vinny walked over to the front doors and swiped his ID in a slot on the wall. The doors buzzed open, and Median was about to say something, when he saw a gaggle of patients—some in wheelchairs, some using crutches, all of them headed in the direction the two of them had just come from.

"Where are they going?" Median asked.

Vinny shook his head. "It's like the War of 1812 all over again. The angels promised to free all the souls here if they fought on behalf of the good guys."

"They just got the memo? The fight is over. Even if they had been on time, I don't think it would have mattered. The angels were decimated."

"That's not what that word mea—never mind. I know they don't stand a chance. You know they don't stand a chance. We can at least use the distraction they'd provide."

As if to underline the fact the patients were fighting a lost cause, one of the men who looked reasonably able-bodied lost the battle with staying upright, tripping over his own feet and hitting the floor hard. The woman in the wheelchair behind him tried steering around him and managed to only run over his legs. He whimpered in pain and rolled over in time for someone with a cane to plant it firmly in his crotch before falling herself.

Median looked at the door. "Do I just…go out?"

"Yeah, man. It's open. No guards to speak of. Nobody's looking at the cameras. Just walk out. It'll be hours, maybe even days, before anybody knows you're gone."

Median wanted more than anything to just go. It was so tempting. But those people. Those poor souls…

"They'll be slaughtered," he said, stepping into the vestibule, looking over his shoulder at them.

"What? Them?" Vinny swiped his badge again to unlock the doors. "Fuck them. They had their chance. They're *dead*."

"I know, but they're about to get into a fight that's already over. It isn't their fault."

"Come on, man. We had a deal, remember? I get you out; you get a message to my girl."

"Yeah, but...not like this." Median shook his head. "We have to stop them."

Vinny looked back and forth between the receding crowd and Median. "Bullshit." He huffed. "Come on."

He left the bucket, and they chased after the mob. They were back in the receiving room to the chapel before Vinny and Median got ahead of them. In the space of time they'd been running, Median realized something more—he couldn't leave. Well, he couldn't leave without doing something about what was going on in there.

Sadly, they easily managed to push the crowd away from the doors.

Median turned to Vinny and said, "I can't leave."

"What?"

"I mean, I have to do something first. I have to stop the wedding."

"Let that crush go, man. She's already lost."

Median shook his head. "Not for her. For him. For the devil."

Vinny's face scrunched up in confusion. "What do you mean?"

"She's using *him*. I don't understand exactly what for, but it can't be good if the *devil* is being manipulated. If it means I have to sacrifice myself, I guess I'm willing to do that."

"What about our deal?"

Median reached into his tuxedo pants and inside his underwear. The tape on the note attached to his taint was really on there and hadn't budged the entire time he'd had it. Median tore it off, taking a dozen or so hairs with it and springing tears to his eyes.

"You take it." He handed the note back to Vinny.

"Me?" Vinny's eyes went distant, and again, Median could see the idea of escape had never crossed his mind. "*Me.*" He slowly nodded.

"Take them with you. I'm sure some kind of posse will come around to round up as many as they can, and that'll give you more time to do what you need to do."

Vinny looked at him with a grim expression and nodded.

"We can't let them go in there," Median said. "They'll be slaughtered."

Vinny nodded. "They'll be like a meal. An amuse-bouche."

"That's not the right wor—never mind. I have to get in there without them."

"Just go around back," Vinny said. "Leave the rest to me." Vinny narrowed his eyes. He took off his cap and began rolling up his sleeves, pushing into the crowd, making his way through them.

Vinny uprighted a three-legged chair. They all watched him when he came back and placed it in front of the double doors of the chapel. He stood on the chair and held up his hands in a calming gesture, nodding to Median.

Median figured that was his signal to make his move, but where was the back?

"We are not men and women," Vinny began, clapping his hands for their attention. He raised his voice gradually to a shout. "We are cowards. We cannot be discouraged! There is no lower point for us!" He raised a fist. "Bravery is the milk of the strong, and that has not ever burnt in veins such as ours."

The mixed metaphor didn't exactly work for Median, but Vinny seemed to be on a roll. Every eye appeared to be on him.

"We lack the liquid of the hero. To be discouraged implies we *ever* had the ichor of warriors in our bones, and I submit to you we do not and *nor have we ever*! Ladies and gentlemen, I say unto you with great heart—flee! *Flee!*"

The crowd roared when Vinny emerged from the other side of them, going back down the long hallway, the way they'd come, with the crowd in tow, his fist still high.

Median looked around and didn't see any other hallway. He didn't know what the hell "the back" was supposed to be, but he was confident if he went searching, he'd get lost and wouldn't be able to make it before the whole thing was over and done with.

Median had supposed the chapel doors were locked but hadn't actually thought to check. He gently pulled on one, and it swung toward him.

As he stepped in, he realized this was the trope of so many sitcoms, where the male lead showed up at the female lead's wedding just in the nick of time to profess his love for her and stop the nuptuals.

Beatricia and the devil stood on the platform, facing one another, with Reverend Fawkes one step above them. Satan had tears flowing from his eyes, and they smiled at each other.

"You may now kiss your bride-*hah*," the reverend said.

Everything. Shook.

Gerald Dean Rice

Chapter 30. One Step at a Motherfuckin' Time

She had no idea how long that had taken, but she was exhausted and completely covered in sweat by the time she got to the next floor. Mary pulled open the fire door and stepped onto the floor proper. She was crampy, sore, hungry again, and she wanted nothing more than to lie down right here and go to sleep. But if she stopped now, she'd never get started again. Since she'd declared war on the forces of evil, this thing had to be seen through, or she'd forever be looking over her shoulder, half god for a fiancé or not.

Mary sneezed. Everything up here was coated in a double-thick layer of dust. She wasn't allergic, but it was too much for even the most insensitive of noses. Mary kept walking forward despite not knowing where she was supposed to go. She spotted what looked like a black arrow painted by hand pointing the way just up ahead. Mary finally made it to the arrow and saw it wasn't exactly black, but old blood.

She looked in the direction the arrow pointed—another one about fifteen yards ahead. Mary shuffled on in that direction and double sneezed, briefly aware she had clots of dust around her shoes but not able to give a shit at the moment.

She eventually passed that arrow and another two before coming to a pair of double doors with the words "Delivery Room" scrawled by what had to have been a single finger.

a lowercase hell

"Let's get this shit over with," she said,
pushing her way through.

There was an immediate difference on this
side. The smell of antiseptic that had been missing
before filled her nose. A single light flickered on
farther ahead, and with the lack of bloody arrows,
she figured that was where she was going. Once
Mary got there, she saw Mrs. Manhorn waiting
inside an operating room, her back turned.

Greenish light from the other side filtered
through Mrs. Manhorn's dress, and Mary saw
something hanging between her legs. She found
herself wondering what it could have been, when
the bag containing Mrs. Manhorn's guts finally
slipped the loose sutures and escaped her stomach
cavity.

The bag spread until a corner of it stuck out
from between her feet, yet Mrs. Manhorn didn't
seem to notice. She went on doing whatever it was
she'd been doing before, her hair bunched up and
haphazardly contained in a surgical cap.

Mrs. Manhorn turned around and faced
Mary. The light left absolutely no doubt—Mrs.
Manhorn was very dead. Her eyes weren't set right
in her head, and they were much too wide, almost
like googly eyes. She wore a mask over her mouth
and nose, which made those creepy rotting globules
in her head the only thing Mary could look at.

"Oh, you're finally here!" Mrs. Manhorn
said with a level of cheer Mary ironically thought
was unnatural for a dead person.

Mrs. Manhorn's voice seemed to come from
somewhere other than her mouth. The bag of guts at

her feet slowly rolled toward the far wall, like there was something still alive inside it.

"Why don't you go ahead and get up on the table so we can begin?"

Mary wasn't so sure how to play this. She still had her gun but seriously doubted anything it could do to the standing corpse would be worse than a broken neck and subsequent autopsy. The table obviously was not for giving birth. It was too industrial, like it was meant for carving up huge quantities of animal carcasses. Too exhausted to think of something better with the extremely limited amount of strength she had left, Mary complied.

She sighed with relief once she was off her feet. And her back! The stiffened muscles throbbed deliciously. *Let the fucking apocalypse come*, she thought. *Just don't make me get* up. The release of tension traveled all the way up to her head, and without meaning to, Mary closed her eyes. She didn't know if she'd drifted off, but when she opened them again, Mrs. Manhorn was standing over her.

The woman's eyelids were gone. As far as Mary knew, that wasn't a thing done in autopsies. Then another contraction hit, and she almost rolled off the table, this one probably one of the strongest. She groaned in pain and put her knees up.

"Looks like that little guy is ready to come out." Mrs. Manhorn said it with a smile in her voice, though Mary wouldn't have been surprised if the woman pulled down her mask to reveal she didn't have lips.

She had a clear line of sight to the little table where Mrs. Manhorn had been standing, and her whole body tensed up with fear. It was a table setting, complete with silverware, an empty wine glass, and a neatly folded napkin.

"Just in time too!" Mrs. Manhorn said.

She was close enough for Mary to punch her. Mary could yank her in by the smock with one hand and smash her face in with the heel of the other. She could—

"*Ohhhhhhh, god!*" Pain tore through Mary the likes of which she'd never felt before. She found herself making tight fists at her sides, reminiscent of when she had to have blood drawn—Mary *hated* needles. Her experience with childbirth was limited to what she'd seen on TV and movies. She had figured it was going to be painful, but this felt like her girl was being ripped out of her pelvis.

"You're already dilating. *Goody!*" Mrs. Manhorn said from somewhere between her legs.

Mary wanted her baby. She'd been wanting a child at least the whole of her adult life. But right in this moment, she didn't care who was going to get this baby out of her. She just wanted it out.

Mary was suddenly drenched in sweat. She had never been claustrophobic, but the feel of her soaking clothes clinging to her was like saturated weight anchoring her to the table.

"She's coming."

Mrs. Manhorn didn't bother with a sheet, and Mary saw the top of the dead woman's head while she peered at Mary's most intimate of intimates.

"Almost here," the talking corpse said.

Mary thought she had a pretty good cycle of breathing going on. It was something to cling to as waves of pain battered her.

"When I say push, you push, okay?"

Mary nodded, her lips pursed when she exhaled. What was happening was beyond her control, and she was eager to get through it. A massive cramp seized her middle, and it was all she could do not to clench every muscle in her body.

"Okay…now," Mrs. Manhorn said after a long moment. "Push!"

Mary squeezed with every fiber of her being, and she felt *something* move. It left a hollow of cold in her middle, and she pushed even harder.

"There, that's it!" Mrs. Manhorn said. "Just a little more."

Mary pushed again, even though she thought she felt empty.

"Yes, yes, yes!"

Mrs. Manhorn came around to her side, holding something in a blanket. She turned so Mary could see.

It was a set of bones.

"No," Mary said in horror. "No, please!"

Mrs. Manhorn appeared to be smiling beneath her mask. "Isn't it beautiful?"

The dead woman went back to the table, where she'd been standing before. She began placing the bones on the plate.

Mary was bewildered. The middle of her body was still a sea of agony, but she was certain she needed to get out of here. Instinct told her so.

She rolled to her side, willing her feet to withstand the weight of her body. Mrs. Manhorn seemed too preoccupied to notice the noise she made. A dynamic had shifted somehow, but Mary was too distressed to identify it. Mary had come up here to defeat an enemy without really knowing.

Mrs. Manhorn was still dead, would always *be* dead. Nothing Mary could do was going to change that. It seemed the dead woman had been sated, so she figured the best thing for her to do was to escape before Mrs. Manhorn paid attention to her again.

Mary fell off the table and landed hard on her knees. Her only thought was to escape, to breathe the air outside of this place. To see something not connected with anything damned. Even though she hadn't stood, her legs were shaky, and her head felt like it was filled with a big ball of cotton. But Mary remained focused on her goal— she was getting out of here.

She looked over her shoulder once to see the back of Mrs. Manhorn, hunching at her little table. Mary didn't know what the dead woman was doing and had no intention of asking. She had bones that had come from god knew where, but Mary was absolutely positive her baby was still inside of her. Maryw didn't have a timer but felt the limited span of time dwindling for her to get out of here. For when her actual baby would be born.

And Mary had no intention of being here when that happened.

Despite feeling just as exhausted as she'd been on her way up, Mary found the strength to stumble toward the door to the stairs. She pushed it open and glanced to her left, at the flight below her. Even though the direction would be easier, it was no less tiring to look at. She stepped all the way in and let the door close behind her.

Mary headed headfirst down the stairs.

She tumbled, tits over tea kettle, feeling each sharp corner catching her body while she rolled until she'd gone down all eighteen steps. Mary stood on shaky legs long enough to get to the second half of the flight and then went tumbling down again, making sure to tuck her head, curling her body as much into a ball as possible, rolling until she was at the bottom of the flight, the wind completely knocked out of her.

Mary wheezed. She was able to get to her hands and knees and crawled toward the door. Mary was completely defenseless and knew it. She was no more capable of offering a fight than a fly.

And then it opened.

Derek stood there, a laceration across his forehead but otherwise intact.

He smiled at her. It was time to go home.

Chapter 31. For All the Stars

Alfred's turn had come and gone, he sensed. But a great deal of power still hung in the air. Somehow, he knew it was supposed to have been him who had died. That he should have been the one impaled on the blade with the angel. Morgan had interceded, had given him the opportunity for whatever happened next to truly be his decision. What he'd seen in the book had been exceeded by this experience, and for the first time in his life, Alfred felt the weight of the story of him lifted from his shoulders. He wasn't under anyone or anything's control. Alfred could finally do whatever *he* wanted.

Hammercock lay a few feet away, his legs twisted together like braided rope. Even though he was in a tremendous amount of pain, he'd still tried to come to Alfred's rescue.

The two of them were wounded, alone, and had no idea what was going to happen next. Daylight abruptly turned into night.

He didn't have to be what he'd been his entire life. He didn't *have* to.

Alfred felt the power just outside of his reach, all around him in the ether. He stretched his arms, reaching with more than his physical body, and took hold of it. In this moment, he knew he could probably do almost anything he desired. He could have vengeance. He could force his way back amongst the living and impose his will. He could murder the world one man, woman, and child at a time and send them all careening to a hell of his own design.

Alfred thought of Mary just then. He had believed he couldn't die at the time, but she had proved him wrong. The tingle of energy began to suffuse with his being, and he knew this was beyond what had come from the dead angel and human. He had cracked open something in heaven, and it had poured over him, saturating him with the building blocks of a god. Alfred had done something that was supposed to be impossible. The almost unfelt channel from her to him, like an umbilicus, throbbed when he pulled that power into himself and reversed its course, feeding that power back to her.

He looked at the man who had had nothing but pure, unadulterated, unconditional love for him from the first moment he'd seen Alfred.

"Angel, I—" Hammercock began to say.

Alfred kissed him as the borders between the two men were simply erased.

Then they simply ceased.

Chapter 32. Red Rocket Pop

"To seal this ceremony, now we would like to allow Darvin's third to say a few words," Reverend Fawkes said.

Everyone was silent after, and Median looked around before realizing they were referring to him. He wasn't sure exactly what to say at the wedding of satan and the woman he'd had a deep crush on. Median had never been in a situation similar to this before. He cleared his throat and looked out at the crowd—a mix of human-looking creatures and unholy horrors.

Median looked directly at Beatricia, tears welling in his eyes. The woman he'd been drawn to more than any other before…The love he'd been so desperate to communicate to her since he'd first seen her had only grown, then welled up, coming out of him as words he had no control of.

"I imagine the nest where
rests your
Rapunzelian heart is an
artfully-guarded secret.
Where many have sought and
Died en route, never realizing
They had gone the wrong
Direction. I hope my aim is high and
true
Where I might pass through
The thicket of doubt proven,
And all query within you
Finding my face eager and bald,

Called and awaiting
Grace in the last trial before
Entry into your den of riches."

There was a long pause of pregnant silence. It was the most heartfelt thing Median had ever said in life to anyone, and he didn't entirely know what it meant. Then somebody giggled. Gradually, everyone began laughing, the sound growing into a roar. Tears streamed from many of their eyes or faces turned red. One man fell off the pew and began rolling around in the aisle. A woman hammered her fist on the empty space next to her. Someone literally crawled up a wall and fell back on the floor.

Even though they were all strangers to Median, it still kind of hurt. This was hell, but laying himself bare and seeing even Beatricia covering her mouth to hide her laugh was painful. Had he been able to take back what he'd just said, he wouldn't have.

Median had been obsessed with this woman since he'd first laid eyes on her at a porn set. It had been about more than sex, although he couldn't have named what it had been about her either then or now. If Median was capable of love, he was certain he was in love with her.

Only, the devil wasn't laughing. Satan locked eyes with him, a fist over his heart and a stoic look on his face. That helped a little while the laughter finally died down and the focus returned to the pastor. Median joined everyone else in looking at the man, a stolid expression on his face.

"And now the fruits."

That seemed innocuous enough. Median didn't know why, but the devil began taking off his tuxedo pants. Beatricia helped balance him while he stood on one leg. He'd gone commando, obviously.

She helped him down onto the floor, and by the time he lay back, he had an erection. Not particularly long, but extremely girthy and very red. It reminded Median of something, but he didn't immediately know what.

There was a long moment of silence. Eventually, Median looked up and saw everyone looking at him.

"What?" he asked.

"This is your part, son," Reverend Fawkes said. "You have to eat the fruit."

"What…fruit?"

Beatricia smiled broadly. "Eat the red rocket pop."

"But he said…" Median began and then thought about it.

The devil had said no one had known what the "fruit" had been in the garden of eden. He'd thought it had been a pomegranate.

Of course, that had left room for him to be wrong.

Now Median imagined Eve in the garden, being tricked into giving the serpent fellatio. And in turn, convincing her husband to give the serpent fellatio. And now it was his turn to do as they had done.

"I'm not—I'm not doin' that."

The crowd gasped.

Beatricia's mouth dropped. "You have to. It's the second to the last part of the ceremony."

"What's the last part?" Median asked.

"Making passionate love to me." She hooked a finger into the neck of her wedding gown and pulled. It fell away, revealing absolute perfection.

Median's whole body responded.

He took in every curve. For a long moment, his eyes lingered over her, and then Median looked at the devil, still lying there on the floor. Was a fleeting moment with her worth *that*? In all his time being sexually active—particularly in porn—he'd never done stuff with a man. Yet, Median found himself wondering if he could actually do it.

"'Kay, wait—" Median's eyes danced between the two of them. "For how long?"

Big red dog penis for the most attractive woman in the universe.

It was as simple as that. And he didn't know which way he was leaning.

Median looked away from Beatricia, to the devil and his pole of doom. He'd had it at the back of his mind during his career in the adult film industry that he might be compelled to do "dude stuff," but he wasn't eager about it. Half the time, he'd been able to get away with telling himself it was the pain and he hadn't gotten into this for that. Other times, he just flat-out had to say guys repulsed him and he wouldn't be able to perform—or relax enough to be performed upon. But this was somehow a situation he had never actually considered.

Blowing a guy had simply never been on Median's radar.

He took a step toward the devil before realizing he had no actual buy-in to do this.

Sex with a woman was something he'd done hundreds of times before. Besides, this was someone else's wedding ceremony, not his. What the fuck did he care if their marriage weren't consummated, if that even had anything to do with what this was? Hell, he'd intended to throw a monkey wrench into the wedding from the moment he'd learned about it. This was his opportunity.

Beatricia pressed her body against his and leaned in to bite his earlobe. "If you don't do it," she said, her breath hot against his skin, making him break out in gooseflesh. "I'll pull all your internal organs out of your ass. Just think about that versus getting to have all of this." She was his height in heels, one leg between his, grinding her hips against him.

Median shivered, her nipples carving across his chest.

Would it be that *bad?* he thought, trying to convince himself.

Median figured it was most likely ceremonial. He probably just had to put it in his mouth, maybe go down on it a couple of times, work the shaft a little, and it would be over. *That* versus *this*. He looked at the devil's new wife, hand on one hip, the other squeezing a breast and looking longingly at him.

Muscles he never used intentionally pulled inside him, and he looked back. He was moving toward the devil, lying prone, when the chapel shook again. Median fell off the step and tumbled to the floor. Satan got up and huddled against his new wife, who wrapped her arms around him.

Run, the devil mouthed, huddling against his wife's bosom just as a large section of the ceiling came down on the demons in the left front row.

Their screams were cut off while Median scuttled to his feet. He looked around, the walls caving in as everyone began to panic. Median didn't take a second to ask the devil what was happening.

Instead, he made a beeline for the chapel doors and pushed his way out. He ran down the long hallway, but concrete and plaster had caved in, blocking the entrance to St. Elo. Median turned in the opposite direction, running as fast as he could, putting distance between himself and the voices of the demons behind him, fleeing the chapel.

More chunks of the building were falling, and Median was dodging left and right, even though they weren't really coming down where he was. He was forced to go through a door and found himself looking up at a stairwell. Median turned to go back, and a block fell in front of the doorway. Without wasting another moment, he dashed up the stairs. He went up a flight and pushed through the door.

It looked familiar, but he didn't stop to consider where he was going. It sounded like the stairs behind him were falling, and Median ran away from the noise. The hallway he was running through was mostly empty, but there was an occasional nurse or patient in a room, panicked or ducked down, waiting for the ceiling to crash around their ears.

He cast a glance over his shoulder. A jagged tear in the floor pursued him. Median picked up his pace and ran around a corner. He finally dove to get out of the path of the growing hole in the floor. When he raised his head, he recognized where he was.

Somehow, he'd made it back to his room. Median quickly got to his feet. Thomas T. Telford rested in the other bed, sipping on a juice box. The old man took it out of his mouth and raised it in salute. Median was still in too much of a state of shock to blink.

"I have to get out of here," he said to the old man.

Thomas T. Telford took a long pull from his juice box, then gestured with it toward the window.

"That's your exit," he said.

Median wanted to ask what the hell he was talking about but instead looked out the window. They were only one story up but, at the same time, impossibly far from the first floor. The ground shook again, and this time, it felt like the whole works was coming down around him.

Thomas T. Telford either didn't notice or didn't care, taking another sip from his juice box.

Median slid the window open, probably doing it wrong because it felt like he'd wrenched his shoulder out of the socket in the process. Once it was wide enough for him to fit head and shoulders through, he got on tiptoe and peered out.

It looked like there were a million feet between here and solid earth.

"What. The. Fuck." Median didn't have time to contemplate beyond those three words.

The floor fell away beneath him. Thomas T. Telford was gone.

Median grabbed onto the windowsill and pulled himself up, kicking all the way. He felt momentum going against him when the wall began to fall inward and into whatever abyss below. He finally dragged most of his body over and pitched himself forward.

Median registered his mouth smacking against the side of the building, concrete scraping against his lips, and then he was in free-fall. He had his eyes closed at first but finally opened them. Freedom was as beautiful as it was terrifying, zooming toward him with a speed he couldn't process fast enough.

There was a giant, painless star of white and then solid, unfeeling black.

Chapter 33. The Beautiful Ones

Mary took the last gurgling sip of her juice box before Derek took it away.

"She's all cleaned up now. Do you want to hold her?" the nurse said, coming back into the room, holding a bundle in a pink blanket.

Despite the exhaustion and soreness of every muscle she had, Mary smiled. "Yes," she said with a croaky voice.

The bulky man came over and gently laid her baby on top of her. She was pale as moonlight and had a headful of curly black hair plastered to her scalp. Her baby looked traumatized, like she'd been through a war herself, and she was absolutely beautiful.

"You know, we never talked about a name," Derek said softly.

She liked the way he said that. Like her baby was his too, even though he knew she wasn't. Mary couldn't wait to marry this man.

"I have absolutely no idea." Mary let herself feel every exhausted muscle finally relaxing.

Derek had found her at the bottom of the stairs and had whisked her away to a proper hospital. By the time they'd gotten there, she'd been completely unconscious, and she'd remained so until well after the baby had been born.

The nurse was still staring at them, big-eyed and smiling, while Mary'd held her perfect little angel. This was what she'd been wanting. The hell she'd gone through had been worth it. Mary couldn't say she'd be willing to go through the whole process again, but she was comfortable believing she didn't regret it.

"I'll be riiiiight back," the nurse said.

Derek was stroking her arm. "The doctor said you can go home later today. Everything was normal, despite, y'know."

"What do you mean, honey?" she asked him.

The nurse came back into the room with another bundle, this time in a blue blanket. His smile was just as wide as before. He walked over to Mary and rested it in the crook of her other arm. It was another baby, an exact replica of the one she was already holding.

"Such sweet little angels," the nurse said, his hands laced together to his chest. He shook his head and retreated from the room. "Beautiful."

"Derek, what the hell?" Mary said.

"What?" he asked.

"There's two of them."

"Yeah. That's kind of what you get when you have twins."

"*Twins*," she said. "What the fu—"

Epilogue

He woke up. The man didn't know where he was or how he'd gotten here. He had a headache like a receding hangover, but his mouth didn't taste like booze. The man sat up and realized he was in the bottom of a bunk bed.

Somebody was snoring above him.

He turned and put his feet on the floor. His bare feet. The man wasn't wearing pants. He had on a suit jacket of some kind and a dress shirt, the tails barely covering his junk.

The man couldn't recall where or what exactly, but he'd been somewhere. Somewhere bad.

The bedroom door was open. He could see perfectly in the dark, so he looked around, spotting a digital alarm clock. It was 3:02 a.m. He stood, swayed a second, then felt the floor solid beneath him. The man stepped out into the hall—three other doors, two of them closed. The third one was to a bathroom.

He went in there. Though he hadn't known it before, as soon as he saw the toilet, he had to take a leak. He aimed and let fly, and it must have gone on for over a minute, several back splashes against his naked shins.

The man flushed, turned to the sink, and got a good look at himself in the mirror. He turned the water on to wash his hands. The face wasn't familiar. But some memories were starting to return to him.

He'd escaped…something. Maybe he was just remembering the remnants of a dream. The man had on the suit jacket and shirt of a tuxedo, with a bowtie undone. He was a medium brown with hazel eyes and a thicket of black curly hair. The face meant nothing to him at all and probably could easily be lost in a crowd. He forced a smile and saw a row of well-manicured teeth and healthy pink gums.

That looked familiar, at least.

He went back into the bedroom and flicked on the light.

"Yo," the man in the upper bunk said. "Turn that off. I'm sleep!"

He glanced about the room before outing the light. That was a strange way of thinking of it. *Outing the light.* He wondered why he'd thought of it that way.

The room didn't appear out of the ordinary: a small desk next to the bunk bed with a kitchen chair pushed up to it, a single dresser about a half-foot shorter than him, a poster of LL Cool J on the wall, a closet door, and another door that looked like it led to a deck outside.

Then the outer wall ripped off.

He pressed himself against the dresser while the bunk bed and the man in it disappeared into the night. Wind blew against his body, but it felt somewhat like a hand wrapping itself around him.

He grabbed the doorway and pulled himself out into the hall.

"Rich?" an older woman said on the other side of another bedroom door. "What's goin' on out there?"

He didn't bother answering. The walls cracked all around him, and the ceiling disappeared into the night sky. He almost fell down the stairs he was standing next to but caught his balance and stumbled his way down.

"Woo!" he heard the woman say before her voice was cut off by the wind.

He turned around on the landing, holding onto the wall and rail as best he could while they disintegrated in his hands. The man fell down the last few steps but bounced up, heading for the front door.

Somewhere inside was a barking dog. He didn't bother looking for it, forcing his way into the small vestibule and twisting the locks on a big, wooden door. The man swung it open and swore at the barred security door he wasn't going to get open without a key. On the other side was an enclosed porch. The flimsy plastic windows and structure broke apart and lifted into the sky, along with a porch swing and chairs.

He pushed frantically at the door, afraid to look at the shattering of wood and plaster he heard behind him. A force knocked him onto his back, and he saw stars. When he sat up, there was nothing between him and outside.

The security door and porch were gone. He stepped closer to where the door had just been and looked down. Jagged shards of wood were below him, but the concrete stairs to the porch four feet away were still intact. He didn't allow himself to think, taking a few steps back and making a running leap for the stairs.

The man overshot, and the wind caught and lifted him. He screamed, although he couldn't hear his voice over the deafening howling. Something sharp scratched at his face and hands and stopped his momentum. He could feel himself swinging back and forth and grabbed onto whatever he felt against him.

The man finally opened his eyes to see the rest of the house ripped out of the ground, chunk by chunk. A car alarm shrieked over the wind, and he heard that dog barking again, this time sounding like it was somewhere over his head.

Then the wind stopped. Like turning off a fire hose.

He swayed in the branches of the tree he was in a few more seconds, long enough to trigger the echo of motion sickness.

The house he'd been in a few minutes ago was completely gone, save for what he guessed had been the basement, open like the socket of a missing tooth. No other houses seemed to have been damaged.

He climbed out of the tree, a few branches whipping him in the face before he got to the ground. The man guessed he'd just experienced a tornado but didn't know one could be so specific.

He felt the car a half second before it landed upside down on the lawn, crushing it beyond recognition, although the alarm still blared. The man flinched and yelped, his voice sounding distant to his still recuperating ears.

As porch lights began to come on and people exited their houses to see what was happening, he realized he had no means of explaining this or who he even was. Staying here for authorities and their eventual questions seemed like a *really* bad idea.

The man ran.

He was absolutely nobody. As even more memories returned to him, he realized the dichotomy between the advantages and disadvantages of not knowing who he was. He could disappear, but someone who knew him might recognize him.

A name came to him, and he figured he had to find this person. A tornado attacking the exact spot where he'd been didn't seem random in the least, and he had to find someone who could help him. All he had to do was find out where he was and then get to *him*. If it was the one name he could remember, he hoped this person would have at least some of the answers.

He had to get to Median.